EQUATOR
AND
SEGREGATION

EQUATOR
AND
SEGREGATION

Brian Aldiss

NEW ENGLISH LIBRARY
TIMES MIRROR

First published in Great Britain by Digit Books
Copyright © 1958 by Nova Publications Ltd.

*

FIRST NEL PAPERBACK EDITION JUNE 1973
Reprinted June 1973
This new edition January 1977

*

NEL Books are published by
New English Library Limited from Barnard's Inn, Holborn, London EC1N 2JR
Made and printed in Great Britain by Hunt Barnard Printing Ltd., Aylesbury, Bucks.

45003041 5

I

EVENING shadows came across the spaceport in long strides. It was the one time of day when you could almost feel the world rotating. In the rays of the sinking sun, dusty palms round the spaceport looked like so many varnished cardboard props. By day, these palms seemed metal; by evening, so much papier mâché. In the tropics, nothing was itself, merely fabric stretched over heat, poses over pulses.

The palms bowed stiffly as Scout Ship AX25 blasted up into the sky, peppering them with another spray of dust.

The three occupants of the ship were rocked back on their acceleration couches for only a few seconds. Then Allan Cunliffe got up, strolled casually over to the port and gazed out. Nobody would guess from his composed face that the ship had just embarked on a hazardous mission.

'At once you begin to love,' he said, looking down at the world with a kind of pride.

His friend, Tyne Leslie, nodded in an attempt at agreement. It was the best, at the moment, that he could do. Joining Allan, he too looked out.

Already, he observed wonderingly, the mighty panorama of sunset was only a red stain on a carpet below them; Sumatra lay across the equator like a roasting fish on a spit. Outside: a starry void. In his stomach: another starry void.

At once you begin to live. . . . But this was Tyne's first trip on the spy patrol; living meant extra adrenalin walloping through his heart valves, the centipede track of prickles over his skin, the starry void in the lesser intestine.

'It's the sort of feeling you don't get behind an office desk,' he said. Chalk one up to the office desk, he thought.

Allan nodded, saying nothing. His silences were always positive. When the rest of the world was talking as it never had before, Allan Cunliffe remained silent. Certainly he had as many mixed feelings about the Rosks as anyone else on Earth: but he kept the lid on them. It was that quality as much as any other that had guaranteed a firm friendship between Allan and Tyne, long before the latter followed his friend's lead and joined the space Service.

'Let's get forward and see Murray,' Allan said, clapping Tyne on the back. Undoubtedly he had divined something of the other's feelings.

*   *   *

The scout was small, one of the Bristol-Cunard 'Hynam' line, a three-berth job with light armament and Betson-Watson 'Medmenham X' accelerators. The third member of the team, its leader, was Captain Murray Mumford, one of the first men ever to set eyes on the Rosks, four years ago.

He grinned at the other two as they came into the cabin, set the autopilot, and turned round to face them.

'Luna in five and a fraction hours,' he said. Once you had seen Murray, you would never forget him. Physically he was no more and no less than a superb specimen of broad-shouldered manhood. Five minutes with him convinced you that he had that extraordinary persuasive ability which, without a word being said, could convert potential rivals into admirers. Tyne, always sensitive to the currents of human feeling, was aware of this magnetic quality of Murray's; he distrusted it merely because he knew Murray himself was aware of it and frequently used it to his own advantage.

'Well, what's the picture?' he asked, accepting a mescahale from Allan, trying to appear at ease.

'With any luck, we'll have a pretty quiet job for your first live op,' Murray replied, as they lit their mescahales. 'The target area, as you know, is Luna Area 101. Luna Intelligence reports a new object outside one of the Roskian domes. It's small and immobile – so far, at any rate. It's outside a dome on the southern perimeter of Area 101, which means it is fairly accessible from our point of view.'

'What's the state of light there now, Murray?' Allan asked.

6

'Sundown in Grimaldi, which contains Area 101, was four hours ago. Intelligence suspect the Rosks may be planning something under cover of darkness; we have imposed a lot of shipping restrictions on their Earth-Luna route lately. So our orders are to slip in from the night side and investigate – obviously without being seen, if possible. Just a quick look over, personal inspection in spacesuits. We should not be out of the ship for more than twenty minutes. Then we streak for home again, heroes all.'

The starry void blossomed up again in Tyne's midriff. Action; this was what he feared and what he wanted. He looked at the lunar map Murray carelessly indicated. One small square of it, low in the third quadrant covering Grimaldi, had been shaded yellow. This was Area 101. Beside it, in the same yellow crayon, one word had been written: Rosk.

Tyne noticed Murray studying his face intently, and turned away, 'World Government made a great mistake in allowing the Rosks a base away from Earth,' he said.

'You were the diplomat when Allan and I were just squaddies in the Space Service,' Murray said, smiling. 'You tell us why Area 101 was conceded to them.'

'The official reason given,' Allan said, stepping in to back up his friend, 'was that while we were being kind to aliens we could not expect a space-travelling race to be pinned to one planet; we were morally obliged to cede them a part of Grimaldi, so that they could indulge in Earth-Moon flight.'

'Yes, that was the official face-saver,' Tyne agreed. 'Whenever it is beaten on any point of an agenda, World Government, the United Nations Council, declares itself "morally obliged". In actual fact, we had rings made round us. The Rosks are so much better at argument and debate than we are, that at first they could talk themselves into anything they wanted.'

'And now the Space Service sorts out the results of the politicians' muddle,' Murray said. It sounded slightly like a personal jibe; Tyne could not forget he had once been in politics; and in his present state of tension, he did not ignore the remark.

'You'd better ask yourself how fine a job the S.S. is doing, Murray. Human-Roskian relations have deteriorated to such an extent this last year, that if we get caught in Area 101, we may well precipitate a war.'

'Spoken like a diplomat!' Murray exclaimed sarcastically.

*   *   *

The three of them spent most of the next four and a half hours reading, hardly speaking at all.

'Better look alert. Put your books away,' Murray said suddenly, jumping up and returning to the cabin.

'Don't mind Murray; he often behaves like a muscle-bound schoolmaster,' Allan said laughing.

Not often, Tyne admitted to himself without bothering to contradict his friend aloud. Murray had drunk with them several times at the Madeka Hotel in Sumatra; his manner then had been far from schoolmasterly. He thought of Murray knocking back carioka till the early hours, rising later to eat with a monstrous appetite, while Allan and Tyne beside him pushed away at the large unappetising breakfasts the hotel provided.

The immediate present eclipsed Tyne's thoughts as the great black segment of moon slid up at them. It was like falling into a smile-shaped hole. Radar-guided, the scout became a tiny, moving chip of a ship again, instead of a little world in its own right.

A few lights gleamed far ahead: Rosk lights, shining up from Area 101.

'Strap in!' Murray said, over the intercom.

They were braking. As deceleration increased, it felt as if they were plunging through water, then soup, then treacle, then wood. Then they weren't plunging at all. They were featherlight. With a bump, they stopped. They were down.

'All change; please have your alien identity cards ready!' said Allan. Tyne wondered how he was feeling, even as Allan smiled reassuringly at him.

Murray left the cabin, walking with something like a swagger. He was pleasantly excited. For him, this was the simple life, with no cares but the present one.

'The radar-baffle's on,' he said. 'No signs of alarm from our friends outside. Let's get into our suits as fast as possible.'

They climbed into the spacesuits. The process took half an hour, during which Tyne sweated freely, wondering all the while if their ship had been sighted by Rosk lookouts. But there was no alternative. The spacesuit is a tool; a bulky, complex, hazardous, pernicketty tool for surviving where one is not meant to survive. It needs endless adjustment before it can be trusted. There was not a spacer in the system who did not hate spacesuits, or envy the Rosks their immeasurably superior variety.

At last they had lashed, strapped, dogged and screwed each other into place. Three monstrous robots bumbled round slowly in the confined space, nearly filling the ship with their bulk; they made with slow, underwater gestures for the hatch. Five minutes later, they were all standing on the lunar surface in complete darkness.

In what were already regarded as the old palmy days, before the Rosks arrived in the system, Tyne had frequently been up to the moon, on pleasure and business. He was not prepared for how bleakly uninviting the place appeared now. In the Grade-A darkness, Grimaldi was a desert of frozen soot.

'We've something less than half a mile to the target dome,' Murray said, his voice a whisper in the headsets. 'Let's move!'

They saw by infra-red extensions. Murray led them along by the crater edge, treading round spines of out-cropping debris. The alien domes became visible as black breasts against sequin-studded silk. Through the little grille of his suit window, Tyne saw the world as a plaster mock-up of a reality too unreal ever to be true. He himself was a pigmy imprisoned in the iron bowel of a robot heading for destruction. Fighting off that irrational sensation, he peered ahead for the strange object they had come to investigate.

Something lay ahead. It was impossible to see what it was. Tyne touched Allan's arm. The latter swung round, and then turned in the direction in which Tyne pointed. Murray paused, making a clumsily impatient gesture to them to come on. Perhaps he feels vulnerable as I do, Tyne thought, sympathetically, pointing again through the blackness for Murray's benefit.

Next second, they were bathed in the ashy glare of a search-light, skewered neatly in mid-gesture.

The light came not from the domes ahead, but to one side, from a point by the crater wall. Tyne just stood there, blinded, knowing they were trapped.

'Drop!' Allan shouted.

'Shoot the light out!' Murray said. His great metal-claw went down piston-fashion to the service pistol, came up levelling the cumbrous weapon, jerked with the recoil. Allan and Tyne heard the shots only as vibrant thuds through Murray's suit mike.

He got the light. It cut off – but already another beam was striking out from the nearest dome, swerving and sending an oval across the ash towards them. Probably they were being fired at, Tyne thought detachedly; you would not know until you were hit. He had his pistol out and was firing too, rather wildly, but towards where the enemy attack would come from.

'Here they come! Make for the ship, Tyne!' Allan bellowed.

As the new searchlight swamped them, Tyne caught a glimpse of moving forms. The Rosks had been lying in wait for them. Then a hammerblow struck his shoulder, sending illuminated pain like a crazy neon system all over his body. Gasping, he heard his suit creak with all the abandon of a falling tree. He was going over . . . and as he went, he had a jigsaw puzzle, upside-down, glimpse of approaching Rosks.

*   *   *

When the Rosks had arrived in the solar system four and a half years before, one unambitious day in March, 2189, an epoch ended, though comparatively few people realised it at the time, Man's time of isolation was over. No longer could he regard himself as the only sentient being in the universe. On his doorstep stood a race superior to him scientifically if not morally.

The shock of the Roskian arrival was felt most severely in those countries which for several centuries had been accustomed to regarding themselves as the world's rulers, or the arbiters of its conduct. They were now in the position of a school bully, who, looking carefully over his shoulder, finds the headmaster standing over him.

The Rosks came in one mighty ship, and a quarter of the world's population quaked in fear; another quarter cheered with excitement; the wiser half reserved judgement. Some of them, four and a half years later, were still reserving judgement. The Rosks were no easier to sum up than Earthmen.

Superficially, a Rosk resembled a man. Not a white man but, say, a Malayan. Their appearance varied from one to another, but most of them had light brown skins, no bridge to their noses, dark eyes. The body temperature was 105.1 degrees, a sign of the hotter planet from which they came.

When the Rosks arrived, Tyne Leslie was the youngest second secretary to an under-secretary to the Under-Secretary of the British Corps of the United Nations Council. He had witnessed the endless fluttering in ministerial dovecotes that went on all over the world as the realities of the Rosk-Man situation became apparent. For the true situation emerged only gradually, while language barriers were being broken down. And the true situation was both complicated and unpleasant.

Man learnt something of the impasse from a yellow-haired Rosk, Tawdell Co Barr, who was one of the first Roskian spokesman on the U.N.C.

'Our mother ship,' he explained, 'is an interstellar vessel housing four interplanetary craft and something more than five thousand of our people, male and female. Most of them are colonists, seeking only a world to live in. We have come from a world you would call Alpha Centauri II; ours is the first interstellar voyage ever made from that beautiful but overcrowded planet. We came to Sol, our nearest neighbour in the vastness of space, seeking room to live – only to find that its one habitable planet is already swarming with men. Although we are happy to meet another sentient race, the depth of our disappointment otherwise cannot be measured: our journey, our long journey, has been in vain.'

'It's a civil speech,' Tyne commented, when he heard it. And other civil speeches followed, each revealing at least one awkward fact about the Rosk visit.

To begin with, these facts almost passed unnoticed among the general run of humanity.

After the first wave of shock had passed round Earth, a tide of optimism followed. The real difficulties inherent in the situation only emerged later. Rosks were heroes; most people managed successfully to hide their disappointment at the lack of bug eyes and tentacles in the visitors. Nor did they worry when Tawdell Co Barr revealed that the Roskian political system was a dictatorship under the supreme Ap II Dowl.

Civility, in fact – an uneasy civility on Earth's part – was the order of the day. The big ship circled Earth inside the lunar orbit, a handful of Rosks came down and fraternised, speaking either to the councillors of the U.N.C. or over tridee to the multitude; or they visited some of the cities of Earth.

In return for his hospitality, they presented men with microfilm books about natural and social life on Alpha Centauri II, as well as specimens of their literature and art, and preserved samples of their flora. But no Earthman was allowed to enter their ship. Scientists, politicians, celebrities, newsmen, all were politely refused admittance, and provided with acceptable explanations.

'Our ship is as inviting as a charnel house,' Co Barr admitted gravely. 'Many of our people died on the journey here. Many are dying now, from dietary and sunlight deficiencies, or from mental illnesses brought about by lifelong incarceration. For we have been exiled for two exhausting generations in the night of space. We can go no further. All we ask, all we beg of you, in your

11

mercy, is a place in which we may rest and recover from our ordeal.'

A place . . . But what place? At first it seemed an almost impossible question; the U.N.C. convened practically without a break for weeks on end. For the first time in centuries, all nations were united – in a determination not to allow the Rosks on to their territory.

In the end, two decisions emerged. First, that the Rosks should be granted an Earth base. Second, where it should be.

Both answers were inevitable. Even Tyne, from his back seat in the debate, saw them coming. In the human attitude to the Rosks lay both fear and envy; even if mercy should permit it, it was impossible to demand of the Rosks that they leave the solar system again. Such a move might provoke them to defiance of man. They might in desperation fight for the land they required. And what weapons they might possess was unknown; indeed, what gifts their science might yield upon more intimate acquaintance was a matter for general speculation.

As for the site of the base, it had to be in an equatorial region. Earth's equatorial belt was about as warm as Alpha II's temperate zone. A site in the middle of Africa might be too inconvenient; a small island might prove too self-contained. The increasingly mighty nation of Brazil would tolerate no Rosks near her borders. After many squawkings, orations, protests and uses of veto, an area of eighty square miles just south of Padang in Sumatra was finally ceded as a Rosk base.

'For this small gift our gratitude is immeasurable,' Ap II Dowl, making one of his rare personal visits, said. There were many who considered his choice of adjective unfortunate – or deliberate.

So the Rosks landed on Earth in their massive ship. It soon became clear that they never intended to leave again; they had had enough of space.

Earth was unwilling to play permanent host. The Rosks, multiplying behind a perimeter they had rapidly fortified, represented a threat no less ominous for being unformulated. Yet how to evict them? It seemed to Earth's statesmen that the only possible line of action was to *nag* the Rosks into leaving.

Unfortunately, the more they scratched the sore, the more it itched.

Nation after nation sent its representatives into Sumatra, to see what could be seen, and to pick up any Roskian secrets, if possible. In the big U.N.C. council chambers in Padang, Man

12

and Rosk haggled and talked, demanded and conceded, bluffed and argued. The situation was at once funny and tragic. That old hope of profiting other than materially by the contact of two races was quite lost to view.

Except on diplomatic errands, Earthmen were not allowed into Rosk base, Rosks were not allowed outside it – yet in practice spies on both sides infringed these laws. Padang became full of spies; nation spying against nation, race against race. The situation became more complex still when, in an attempt to ingratiate themselves, the U.N.C. ceded the small Lunar Area 101 to the visitors, to allow them to test out their four interplanetary ships.

'This move touches my heart,' Tawdell Co Barr declared. 'We came as strangers; you welcome us as friends. Together, Rosk and man will build a new and lasting civilisation.'

By this time, such fair words rang hollow.

Whether Tawdell meant it or not, the hopes he expressed were the hopes of many men, everywhere. Unfortunately, this was Tawdell's last public speech! He disappeared into the Rosk base and was not heard of again. It was believed in diplomatic circles that the yellow-haired Rosk had been too friendly towards man for his overlords' liking. Ap II Dowl's dictatorship, which had been formed in the harsh environs of the ship, now took the reins. His henchmen sat at the council tables, and relations between the two sides slowly deteriorated.

The spy patrol in which Murray, Allan and Tyne served was only one instance of that deterioration.

II

SOMETHING like a lemon. No, a melon. No, it was stretching; a cucumber. No, it was bending; a banana. No, curling; a slice of melon. No, a melon again. Or was it – it was all distorted – was it a face? It rippled, solidified. It took on a firm jaw and eyes staring fixedly down. It became Murray Mumford's face, seen through a haze of weakness.

'Oh!' groaned Tyne. He was in a bunk which still rippled at the edges, staring up at Murray.

'How is it?' Murray asked. 'Feeling better?'

'Drink of water,' Tyne said.

He gulped it down when it was brought. His head cleared. He remembered the incident at 101, the numbing blow on his spacesuit.

'Where are we, Murray?' he asked.

'One hour out from Lunar, unpursued, heading back home,' Murray told him. 'I was too quick for the Rosks. I thought you were never coming round. How do you feel?'

'This is the best part of me.' Tyne said ironically, raising his gloved left hand. Beneath the glove were substitute steel fingers and palm: his real hand had been amputated after an air crash several years ago.

'I don't think there's much more wrong with you,' Murray said, 'apart from a few bruises. The Rosks fired on us. A bullet hit your suit glancingly on the shoulder; luckily no joints split, and shock absorbers took most of the blow. How do you do it – magic rabbit's foot?'

'How did I get here? Didn't I black out?'

14

'You blacked out all right, went down like a felled ox. I part-dragged, part-carried you here,' Murray said. 'Fortunately, as you went down I managed to shoot out the second Rosk searchlight.'

'Thanks, Murray,' Tyne said, and only then, with a rush of guilt, remembered his friend. 'Where's Allan?'

Murray turned away, drawing his thick brows together as if in pain. 'I'm afraid Allan didn't make it,' he said quietly.

'How do you mean, didn't make it?'

Swinging back to the bunk, as though he had suddenly found the words he wanted, Murray said, 'Look, Tyne, this may be difficult for you to take. Things got out of hand back there. It was a nasty spot – you know that. When you went down, I grabbed you and got you over one shoulder. Allan shouted out to me to run for it and leave you there. It must have been a moment of panic, I suppose. He wanted to leave you for the Rosk. I told him to cover my retreat, and the next thing I knew, he was waving his gun in my face, telling me he'd shoot me if I did not drop you!'

'Allan!' Tyne protested. 'Allan said that?'

'Have you ever panicked?' Murray asked. 'There are situations when your moorings break loose, and you don't know what you are saying or doing. When I saw Allan's gun in my face, and felt the Rosks coming up behind, I – I lost control of what I was doing, too.'

He turned his head again, his big body tense in a way Tyne had never seen it before. The man on the bunk felt his mouth go dry as he asked. 'What did you do, Murray?'

Space slid by outside, sly, snakey, cold as time at a crisis, ignoring Murray as he said, 'I shot Allan. Right in the stomach.'

Tyne was bound down on his bunk. He could only wave his steel fist and his flesh fist, impotently.

'There was nothing else to do,' Murray said savagely, clutching one of the waving wrists. 'Listen to me, Tyne, should I have left you there, out cold? We weren't supposed to be in Area 101 – we had no legal right. Would you rather have come to with a group of killer Rosks round you? I did the only thing I could. Allan Cunliffe mutinied; as captain, I dealt with it on the spot. There's no more to it than that.'

'But I know Allan,' Tyne yelled. 'How could he – he wouldn't – he's not the sort –'

'We none of us know each other,' Murray shouted back. His face was dark, suffused with a feverish look of excitement. 'We

15

don't even know ourselves. In a moment of crisis, something takes over from us – our id, or something. That's what happened to Allan. Now shut up, and think things over till you see I did the only possible thing.'

He strode forward into the cabin, slamming the door behind him, leaving Tyne alone.

Tyne lay where he was, churning the whole thing over in his brain. He could believe neither that his friend was dead, nor that he had lost control of himself. Yet he could not do other than believe; after all, submerged rivalry for promotion had always existed between Allan and Murray; perhaps in those frightening seconds in the dark, it had come to a head.

Once before they landed, Murray returned to the crew room, to look in at Tyne. His manner was still tense.

'How are you feeling now?' he asked.

'I don't want to see you,' Tyne said grimly. 'I'll see you at the court of inquiry. Till then, keep out of my way.'

His face setting into harsh lines, Murray came across to the bunk and put his hand over Tyne's throat.

'Watch what you're saying and who you're saying it to,' he said. 'I've told you the facts. I don't like them any better than you do. If Allan had not suddenly turned coward, he'd be here with us now.'

Tyne brought his steel left hand over, clasping the other's wrist, squeezing, squeezing. Letting out a gasp of pain, Murray pulled his arm away; a bracelet of red flesh encircled it. He allowed Tyne one look of malice, then went back and shut himself in the cabin. It was the last Tyne would see of him for a surprisingly long while.

*　　*　　*

When they landed, Tyne lay patiently for a time, then bellowed for Murray to come and release him. Webbed straps, fastening under the bunk, ensured that he could not release himself. No answer came to his shouts. After twenty minutes, the rear air lock opened, and two Sumatran medical orderlies entered with a stretcher.

From them, Tyne gathered that he was back at Patrol H.Q. Murray had phoned straight through to the hospital, telling them to collect him from the scout for examination.

'I'll come round for examination later,' Tyne said, testily. 'Right now, I have to report to the Commander.'

16

'Don't worry; the Commander has already been informed about the state of your health,' one of the orderlies said.

Despite Tyne's protests, the man was adamant. From his replies, it seemed as if Murray had cast some doubts on Tyne's sanity. So Tyne was carted to the military hospital on a stretcher.

Procedure there was no more rapid than in any other hospital. It took the doctors a long while to decide that Tyne Leslie was sane but savage, bruised but sound. In between the examinations were periods of waiting. All this, Tyne thought angrily, smoking his way through a packet of mescahales, was Murray's doing: the scout captain had fixed this so that Tyne's report was delayed. Well, he would fix Murray. Murray was going to be in trouble.

After two hours, buttoning up his uniform, he hurried over to Squadron Office. There a surprise awaited him. Murray had not reported in from his mission. Murray had not been seen. Suspicion and curiosity brewing in his mind, Tyne hurried over to the billets where the squadron lived. Nobody there had seen Murray either; his room was empty, none of his kit disturbed. Over his bed, a pretty half-caste girl stared saucily, blankly, from her photograph. Written in babyish letters across it were the words 'Love from Mina.'

The sun was gathering its full, mid-morning glory about it. Ignoring it, Tyne ran to the main gate to question the traffic cop on duty under his concrete umbrella. Yes, Captain Mumford had left in a staff car just after breakfast, heading for town.

'Thanks,' Tyne said. He thumbed a lift into town himself, riding the five miles of dust and sunshine in grim impatience.

He knew he should have reported in properly before leaving camp; above all he should have reported Allan's death. But in an obscure way he felt time to be vital. Murray had inexplicably disappeared; it would be easier to find him while the trail was hot. The time was 10.50.

*　　*　　*

Padang was one of the most interesting cities on Earth. To every layer of its life, the nearness of the Rosk base gave an agreeable frission of excitement. The feelings that something gigantic might happen any day hovered over its hot, scented streets. It was an international city. Among the native Indonesians and Chinese moved U.N.C. delegates from all over the Earth, or their wives, mistresses or followers. Street vendors hawked national emblems of every conceivable kind, from rising suns to leeks. It was also an inter-system city, the first on Earth, for Roskian U.N.C. delegates, prominently displaying their lapel permits, strolled through the city or sat at restaurants. It was, above all, a boom city. Along the gay Tida Appa, skyscrapers rose. Among the palms, the shanties, the picturesque two-storey streets: solid blocks of flats rising. Above the crowds: fifty different flags drooping in the heat.

After the politicians came the business men; after the business men, the underworld. By winking through your hotel window, you could buy yourself a lawyer, a woman, or a long float, face down, in the sewers.

Dropped in the centre of town, outside the post office, Tyne slipped thought the great undercover market, and headed up Bukit Besar. He entered the Merdeka Hotel. It seemed to him the obvious first place to look for Murray. The Merdeka had been the nearest equivalent to home for Allan, Tyne and Murray. They had grown to love its efficient service, its poor food, its constant bustle.

The place was full now, mainly with the sort of minor diplomatic staff Tyne had once been; nervous, cheery men downing their whiskies and keeping out of the sun – and waiting, waiting and watching. Pushing through the hall, Tyne went round the back way, to the back stairs.

He thought he saw Amir at the end of the passage, looking round and then dodging out of sight. But that could not be. Amir, the brightest boy on the staff, would have no reason to hide in that way; he had become almost a personal friend of theirs.

Climbing the back stairs, fishing his key out of his pocket as he went, Tyne reached Room Six. This was the room Allan, Murray and Tyne shared. Had shared . . . Unlocking the door, he went in.

The immense influx of foreigners had caused a housing shortage in Padang. Hotel rooms were impossible to find; only by paying through the nose for this one all the time did they enjoy the privilege of using it at weekends.

A hurricane had hit Room Six.

Tyne whistled. All their kit, their civilian clothes, everything, had been flung into the middle of the floor. Someone had searched the place, thoroughly, in a hurry. Who? Why?

'I don't like it,' Tyne said aloud. He went and shouted over the banisters for service.

As he waited, he stood in the middle of the room, thinking. He was involved in a mystery. Something odd had happened on the moon – he had not heard the truth about that, he felt sure.

18

Now something odd had happened here. Why had Murray deserted? Where had he gone? A numbing suspicion that he had murdered Allan overtook Tyne. But why?

He went back on to the landing and shouted for service again.

Hatred for Murray filled him. It reached back, embracing Murray-in-the-past. The big man's easy manner now seemed no longer likeable, but the sign of a boundless superiority. His ready, cheerful smile became false, the arbitrary grimace of a murderer. Yet supposing he had killed Allan . . . he could so easily have told Tyne that the Rosks had shot him – Tyne, after all was unconscious when it happened. Nothing was sure. Rather, one thing was sure: Tyne wanted to get hold of Murray and wring the truth out of him.

He went out on to the landing to bellow for service again, and nearly bumped into a little maid.

'Where's Amir?' Tyne asked.

'Amir has a day off today.'

'What? First time I've ever known him have a day off.'

'Amir is not so well today. Had a bad head and takes medicine. What I can get for you?'

Suddenly, he wanted nobody to see into the room. He felt weak, tired, hungry; this was his first man hunt.

'Will you bring me some breakfast, please?'

'Breakfast is long finish, sir.'

'Make it lunch then, anything.'

Going back into the room, he locked the door on the inside. He started methodically tidying the muddle on the floor. It hurt to fold up Allan's belongings, knowing he would not want them again. Some of Murray's civilian clothes were missing, but a uniform was here. So.

Lunch came promptly, a denationalised dish of chopped sausage, cabbage and rice, followed by tasteless plankton jelly. A big new plankton plant down the coast at Semapang provided more and more food for the island; as yet, its products were more nourishing than appetising.

With the meal, Tyne's spirits rose. He had ceased to be a second secretary to an under-secretary of the Under-Secretary because he wanted action. Here it came. The original instinct that had led him to Sumatra had been sound. He had been static, stale, discontented, a man without manhood, set on a career of his father's choosing that bored him thoroughly. His chief task had been minute passing: how suitable that that should be a synonym for time wasting!

19

But the equator is the hottest bit of the planet, the bit that goes round fastest, though that is not apparent to the senses. Now something was really starting to spin.

On his way out, he ran into the proprietor and asked for Murray.

'Sorry. I don't see him today,' Mr Niap Nam said. 'If he come, I don't see him. Now it is best for you to leave by the back way. In front is having a little trouble from the Displaced. Maybe shooting from these foolish men.'

'Thanks, Niap,' Tyne said. He had heard the noise in the street but had taken no notice of it. In a moment, one shot was fired, the shouting rose to a crescendo, then came the sound of people running. Tyne slipped out the back way, through the courtyard, under the cassia tree. The Displaced were a group of terrorists, largely formed from natives whose kampongs had been evacuated to make room for the Rosk base: their daily acts of violence – often the sticky-bombing of diplomats' limousines – added an additional spice of risk to life in Padang.

*   *   *

Tyne headed for the Roxy. If anyone knew where Murray was, it should be Mina, the little half-Dutch girl (her other half remained unspecified) who occupied most of Murray's spare time. Tyne looked at his watch. It was just after noon; his enemy, for already that was how he thought of Murray, had as much as four and a half hours' start.

The Roxy was an all-day cinema. Now the boom was on, the solids flickered in the big perspex cube for twenty-four hours out of the twenty-four. The foyer was large, deep, lush, with people coming and going, or just standing smoking.

On the ice cream counter, Mina squeaked with pleasure at the sight of Tyne. Yes, she was nice: dark, lively, animated; perhaps after Murray was out of the way . . .

'Yes, he came to see me here,' Mina said, in answer to Tyne's question. 'Is he in some sort of trouble, Mr Leslie, can you tell me? He had a look as if something is striking him not so funny.'

'Perhaps he had his shoes on the wrong feet,' Tyne said, and then waited patiently for the girl to control her shrieking laughter. He had forgotten how the silliest remark set her going.

'I've got to find him, Mina,' he said. 'The Commander wants him urgently. Did he say where he was going?'

'No, Mr Leslie. All he say is not even "give a kiss" but just "hello". That is why I think perhaps something is striking him not –'

'Yes, not so funny. I know. What else did he say besides "hello", Mina? Did he ask you to meet him later?'

'Excuse a minute.' She turned, all smiles, to serve a tall Pakistani, and then continued, 'All he say to me is that he goes to the plankton plant. I can find him at the plankton plant. What for he wants to go to that place for, Mr Leslie?'

'Perhaps to plant plankton,' Tyne suggested, turning away unsmiling as she doubled up again with fluty laughter. What the devil would Murray be going out there for? Walking blindly, he almost bumped into a fat man in a white linen suit.

'Follow me to hear about Murray Mumford,' the fat man said; speaking from the corner of his mouth and appearing to take no notice of Tyne. As Tyne stared after him in surprise, the fat man pushed through a swing door into one of the adjoining bars. For a moment, Tyne wondered if he had heard all right. Then he shouldered his way through the door.

*　　*　　*

A miniature solid a foot high fluttered on the bar counter. It was silent. Piped from the full-size cinema solid, it showed only half the original. As such, it was almost unintelligible: but its job was to lure bar-flies inside to see what the original was about. At present, the breasty half of Lulu Baltazar reclined on pillows gesturing meaninglessly.

Tyne flicked his gaze from the cube to the fat man. The fat man was sitting in the far corner with his face to the door, raising two plump fingers to the waiter. The waiter was nodding and smiling like an unctuous fool. Several people sat about, drinking.

'Who are you?' Tyne asked the fat man, on reaching his table. 'Sorry, but I don't remember you.'

'Sit down, Mr Leslie,' the stranger said. 'Remember your manners and thank your lucky stars I found you before anyone else did.'

'Who are you, I asked?' Tyne said, sitting down. 'Have you a message for me from Murray?'

'Here come the whiskies,' the other said, smiling as the waiter set the glasses down. 'Let me drink to your continued health.'

Tyne pushed his away.

'I'm in a hurry,' he said. 'How do you know I am after Murray?

I suppose you overheard what I said to the ice cream kiosk girl? Are you trying to be funny or helpful?'

The fat man downed his drink and then, looking quizzically at Tyne, usurped the one Tyne had pushed away. Without troubling to answer any of Tyne's questions, he said, 'If you want to call me anything, Stobart is as good a name as any, I'm a U.N.C. agent. I can arrest you by flicking my fingers, should I feel like it.'

A bit – a very nice bit – of Lulu Baltazar was climbing into a dynocar. The waiter was smiling and nodding like a fool to new patrons.

'You talk as if you've just popped out of a cloak-and-dagger solid,' Tyne said.

'Don't reveal your genteel background, son,' Stobart said curtly, 'I'm real enough, as you'll find out if you start playing tough. And remember – I've got no sense of humour.'

'All right. You're real,' Tyne conceded. 'Then tell me this. Why should a U.N.C. agent reveal himself as you have done? Why should he be interested in me, or in Mumford? If you were a thick-eared M.P. from camp, I could understand it.'

'You couldn't understand a thick-eared hatstand. Look, son, you are dabbling on the edge of deep waters. Stay out. That's all I'm here to tell you; stay out! The finding of Murray Mumford is top priority, and you'll only be in the way of several interested parties.'

As he spoke, he slid the whisky back to Tyne, who took it and drank it. Stobart raised two fingers in the air, and the waiter doubled over, curtseying, with more drink.

'Let me in on the mystery,' Tyne said. He disliked the note of pleading he heard in his own voice. 'Why did Murray kill Allan Cunliffe? Why are the U.N.C. and not the police or the Space Service after him?'

'You're inquisitive,' Stobart said stonily.

Tyne went red in the face. He took one of the empty glasses in his left hand and squeezed. He went on squeezing till a little pile of glittering fragments lay on the table.

'Answer my questions,' he said.

Stobart laughed. 'You've got a temper,' he said, and blew the powdered glass over Tyne's jacket. Before Tyne could move, the other had grasped his left wrist in an unshakable grip.

'Listen to me, Mr Leslie,' Stobart said. 'Stay out of this. Mumford lied to you, I don't doubt. He wouldn't let you see how big this thing was. I want to hear what he told you happened outside Area 101; then I'll tell you what really happened. Fair enough?'

Sullenly, Tyne repeated the story Murray had told him on the scout ship.

'Hogwash,' Stobart exclaimed at the end of it. 'While you were out cold on the moon, the Rosks *caught* you and Mumford. He had no time to get back into the ship, man, not with you sleeping peacefully on his shoulder. They caught him as easy as kiss your hand, and persuaded him to carry vital information down here, to a Rosk contact in Padang who will pass it to the Rosk Sumatra base.'

'How could they persuade him? What was the information? Why couldn't he have told me the truth?'

'You innocent fool!' Stobart said. He had stopped looking at Tyne now, as if he had lost interest in him; his watery eyes slid round the other customers in the bar. 'Do you think Mumford would tell anyone the truth? He has turned traitor! He's helping the Rosks; don't bother to ask me what they offered him for the job. And don't bother to ask me what the information is; if I knew I shouldn't tell you.'

'I can't believe it! Why couldn't the Rosks carry the information themselves? They've got four small ships plying between Earth and Luna.'

'If we knew all the answers, we'd not be looking for Mumford now,' Stobart said tersely. 'And that's all I've got to say to you. On your way, Leslie, blow. Go back to camp and play spacemen before the shooting starts.'

'You're drunk, from the way you talk and look,' Tyne said quietly. 'Or does your mouth always hang down like an old red sock?'

'There's a Rosk sitting up at the bar disguised as a Sumatran business man, watching us like a hawk,' Stobart replied, without batting an eyelid.

'I'm from Neptune,' Tyne said. 'How did you get hold of all this information, Stobart?'

The fat man swore at him. 'Think I'd tell you? For the last time, get, Tyne. You're up against organisations. You'll never find Murray Mumford. Go on, on your feet, beat it! The free whisky is finished.'

A bit of someone was wrestling with a bit of Lulu Baltazar as Tyne passed the bar. He boiled inside. His face burned. He hated every cubic inch of lard in Stobart's body, but his intelligence told him the man's advice was sound. If Murray was really

23

involved in trouble so deeply, the affair had passed out of Tyne's hands.

Avoiding Mina's eye, he strode out on to the Roxy's steps. It was raining heavily. The streets ran with water. Further up the street, two miserable policemen stood beside a smoking Russian Pudenta; the Displaced had struck again. The time was 1.15.

Inside the cinema, Stobart watched with satisfaction as the Rosk agent slid from the bar and left, almost directly after Tyne Leslie. Stobart liked his job. As long as you stayed in control it was as comfortable as an old armchair. With the right psychological push, anyone could be induced to do anything. Even a random factor like Mr Tyne Leslie.

III

TYNE decided to cut through the side streets. He might dodge most of the rain that way. The sooner he got back to base, the better; there would be trouble awaiting him for failing to report in from a completed mission. He felt full of defeat. He had even forgotten to ask that slob Stobart about Allan.

Rain pelted down his neck. His light tropical suit would be soaked in no time. A taxi slowly overtook him, splashing his legs.

'Jump in for a good ride, sir,' the Chinese driver called cheerfully.

It was a sound idea. As Tyne bent to open the back door, it was flung wide. Strong hands grasped his hand, catching him off balance, pulling him into the car. He felt it gather speed even as he struggled under a heavy rug which was thrown over him. Someone was lying on top of him, pinning him down. Tyne fought to get his steel hand free. Then a blow caught him on the nape of his neck.

For what seemed like an eternity, he lay half-suffocating under the rug, in a drifting state between consciousness and unconsciousness. Lurid colours curled and coiled in his head. When the car began to bump, as if it had left the road, he took an intelligent interest in the world again. An odd hissing noise rose outside; they were driving through long grass.

The occupant of the back of the car had climbed off Tyne now, and was arguing with the driver. It was something about damage to the machine. Money was offered, the driver was refusing it.

At length the car stopped. Tyne did not struggle as his wrists were lashed behind his back. The hands that touched his felt feverishly hot. Undoubtedly their temperature was 105.1 degrees.

He was hauled unceremoniously out of the car by his shoulders, rolling over in knee-deep, wet grass. As he struggled to his knees, and then to his feet, he saw the Chinese driver accept a wad of dollars, grin and rev the engine. The Rosk took Tyne by the belt of his pants, pulling him out of the way as the car backed round and shot back up the track in the direction it had come from. It disappeared; man and Rosk were alone.

Tall trees, secondary growth rather than true jungle, surrounded them. The only sign of human existence was an old native hut sagging under its own weight, although in the distance came the regular sound of traffic: a highway not too far off.

'Let's walk, shall we?' the Rosk said, pleasantly, pushing Tyne ahead.

'If you've nothing better to offer.'

It was still raining, but without passion, as they started down the track. Tyne had hardly managed to get a glimpse of his assailant. He looked like a Malayan. How ironic, Tyne thought, that this race should have set itself up in Sumatra! They could pass anywhere here unnoticed. In England, they would stand out a mile.

'Fond of the country?' Tyne asked.

'Keep walking.'

The track grew worse. The rain stopped as if a celestial tap had been turned off. The sun came out; Tyne steamed. Through the trees, the ocean appeared. It lay there flat as failure, stagnant and brassy.

The cliffs were steep here, deep water coming in close. Together, Tyne and his captor slithered down a perilous slope. At the bottom, three great palms fought motionlessly for position on a minute ledge, their stony trunks canting over the water. Down below the surface, their roots extended like drowned fingers; Tyne could see fish among the fingers. Then, without warning, he was pushed off the ledge.

He went down among the roots, the water burning up his nose. He struggled frantically. He was drowning! With his hands tied, he was helpless.

There was hardly time to think. The Rosk was swimming beside him, tugging his collar. In no time, they slid into darker water under the cliff, and surfaced. Water streaming from his mouth and clothes. Tyne gasped painfully, floundering up rough steps as the Rosk dragged him out.

26

They were in a cavern, the mouth of which would be hardly visible even from the sea, thanks to the big palms outside. Conditions were claustrophobic in the extreme. The water came within two-foot six of the slimy roof; there was no chance of climbing out of the water – one just stood chest deep in it. Bitterly, Tyne remembered that the Rosks had strong aquatic traditions.

In the middle of the cavern, in deeper water, floated a small submarine. It looked battered and ancient, and was streaked with rust. It might have been a veteran from the Malayan Navy, but Tyne could not certainly identify it.

The conning tower was open. A dark head now appeared, exchanging a few barked words with Tyne's captor. Without delay, he was prodded aboard.

Inside, it was like crawling round an oven, both as regards heat and size. Tyne was made to lie on the bare steel lattice of a bunk, his hands still tied behind his back. When the sub began to move, the motion was barely perceptible.

Shutting his eyes, he tried to think. No thought came. He only knew that the repulsive Stobart's warning had been well founded but too late. He only knew that he coveted the life of a second secretary to an under-secretary of the Under-Secretary.

'Up again now,' the Rosk said, prodding his ribs.

They had arrived.

Pushed and goaded from behind, Tyne climbed the steel ladder and thrust his head into daylight.

The sub had surfaced out to sea. No land was visible, owing to haze which hung like a steam over the smooth water. A native, low-draught sailing ketch floated beside them, a mooring line from it already secured to the sub's rail. Three presumed Rosks showed predatory interest when Tyne appeared. Reaching over, they took him by his armpits and hauled him aboard, to dump him, dripping on deck.

'Thanks,' Tyne snapped. 'And how about a towel, while you're feeling helpful?'

When his first captor had climbed aboard, he was urged down a companionway, still dripping. Below decks, structural alterations had created one good-sized room. The ketch was perhaps a hundred-tonner. Evidence suggested it had been used as a passenger boat, probably to nearby islands, before it passed into Rosk hands.

Five male Rosks and a woman were down here. They were dressed in Rosk style, with a abundance of oily-looking cloth over them that seemed highly out of place on the equator. Relaxed here, among their own people, the *foreign-ness* of them became more apparent. Their mouths, perhaps by the quick, clattering language they spoke, were moulded into an odd expression. Their gestures looked unnatural. Even in the way they sat on the plain wooden chairs was a hint that they found the artifacts alien, out of harmony.

These were beings from Alpha Centauri II, beings like men, but inevitably always estranged from man. The physical similarity seemed merely to mark the spiritual difference. As though life on Earth, Tyne thought, wasn't complicated enough without this. . . .

The Rosk who had captured Tyne in Padang was delivering a report, in Roskian, to the leader of the group, a coarse-looking individual with nostrils like a gorilla's and a shock of white hair. He interrogated Tyne's captor at length, searchingly, but in a manner that suggested he was pleased with the man, before turning to address Tyne in English.

'So now. I am War-Colonel Budo Budda, servant of the Supreme Ap II Dowl, Dictator of Alpha-Earth. We need information quickly from you, and shall use any means to extract it. What are you called?'

'My name is Pandit Nehru,' Tyne said, unblinkingly.

'Put him on the table,' Budda said.

Moving in unison, the other Rosks seized Tyne and laid him, despite his struggles, heavily on his back in the middle of the table.

'Pandit Nehru was a figure in your history,' Budda said impatiently. 'Try again.'

'Martin Todpuddle,' Tyne said, wondering just what they did or did not know about him.

Evidently they did not know his name.

'You were talking to a U.N.C. agent,' Budda said, 'at half-past twelve by your local time, in the Roxy Cinema, Padang. What were you talking about?'

'He was telling me I should change my socks more often.'

A terrific side-swipe caught Tyne on his right ear. The world exploded into starlit noise. He had forgotten how unpleasant pain could be; when he reclaimed enough of his head to render hearing partly possible again, a lot of his cockiness had evaporated.

Budda loomed over him, gross, engrossed.

'We people from Alpha II do not share your ability for

28

humour,' he said. 'Also, time is very vital to us. We are about to select from you a finger and an eye, unless you tell us rapidly and straightly what the U.N.C. agent spoke about to you.'

Tyne looked up from the table at their foreshortened faces. What were these blighters thinking and feeling? How did it differ from what men would think and feel, in their position? That sort of basically important question had never been intelligently asked or answered since the Rosks arrived, nearly five years ago. The great, seminal, emancipating event, the meeting of two alien but similar races, had been obscured in a fog of politics. The merging of cultures boiled down to a beating-up on a table.

Tyne had been on the talking end of politics. Now here he was on the receiving end.

'I'll talk,' he said.

'It's a wise choice, Todpuddle,' Budda said; but he looked disappointed.

This acceptance of his false name gave Tyne heart again. He began a rambling account of the murder of his friend Allan, without saying where it took place.

Within a minute, the Rosk who had captured Tyne came forward, clattering angrily in Roskian.

'This fellow says you lie. Why do you not mention Murray Mumford?' Budda asked.

Turning his head, Tyne glared at his first captor. He had had no chance until now to get a good look at him. Like a shock, recognition dawned. This was the man drinking at the bar of the Roxy, whom Stobart had named as a Rosk agent; he was still dressed as a local business man. Then if Stobart knew this fellow, perhaps Stobart or one of his men was following, and already near at hand. Perhaps – that thought sent his flesh cold – Stobart was using, him, Tyne, as bait, expecting him to pass on Stobart's tale to the enemy. Stobart, as a rough calculation, was as callous as any three Rosks put together, even allowing two of them to be Ap II Dowl and Budo Budda.

His mind totally confused, Tyne paused.

At a barked command, one of Budda's henchmen began to rip at Tyne's clothes.

'All right,' Tyne said. One look at Budda, crouching eagerly with tongue between teeth, decided him. 'This is what Stobart said.'

While they stood over him, he told them everything, concealing only the fact that he had been personally involved in the

29

affair on Luna. As he talked, Budda translated briskly into Roskian.

On one point in particular the War-Colonel was persistent.

'Stobart told you Mumford had to meet one of our contacts in Padang town, you say?'

'That's right.'

'Mumford did not have to go to our base here?'

'I can only tell you what Stobart told me. Why don't you go and pick up Stobart?'

'Stobart is not so easily caught as you, Todpuddle. There is a native saying of ours that little fish are caught but big fish die natural deaths.'

'Stuff your native sayings. What are you going to do to me?'

Budda did not answer. Going over to a cupboard, he opened it and pulled out a simple-looking gadget that evidently functioned as a radio phone. Something in his manner of speaking into it suggested to Tyne that he was addressing a superior, presumably at Sumatra Base. Interestedly Tyne sat up on the table: nobody knocked him flat again. The interrogation was over.

Replacing the instrument, Budda began shouting orders to the other Rosks.

Tyne slid his feet down on to the floor and stood up. His clothes were still wet, and clung to him. The cords that secured his hands behind his back seemed to grow tighter by the minute.

'Are we going home now?' he asked.

'You are going to your eternal home,' Budda said. 'You have served your function usefully, Mr Todpuddle, and I am grateful. Now we all go to capture Mumford in a big hurry, leaving the lady of our party, Miss Benda Ittai, to sew you in a sack and hurl you in the blue water. It is an ancient Alpha form of burial. Farewell!'

'You can't leave me like this –' Tyne shouted. But the others were already hurrying up the companionway. He turned to face the Rosk woman.

He already knew she was beautiful. That was something he had noted instinctively on entering, although his mind had been on other things. Now he saw how determined she looked. Benda Ittai was small but wiry, very graceful despite her strange clothes, and she carried a knife – an Indonesian blade, Tyne noted.

She came towards him warily, clattering brusquely in her native tongue.

'Don't waste your breathe, Mata Hari,' Tyne advised. 'I can't savvy a word of it.'

He could hear the others climbing down into the sub; they'd be packed in there like kippers in a can he thought. When they had gone, he could rush this little thug, knock her over, and get free.

But the little thing knew her onions. Bringing out an old sail from a locker, she spread it on the deck. Moving swiftly, she got Tyne in a sort of Judo hold and flung him down on top of the sail. Before he knew what was happening, he was rolled into its folds. Struggling was useless. He lay still, panting, to listen. Benda Ittai was sewing him in – very rapidly, with an automatic needle. Right then, he really grew frightened.

When she had rendered him quite harmless, she went up on deck. In a minute she was back, tying him round the middle with rope and thus dragging him, bump by bump, up the narrow stair well. The stiff canvas protected him from the harder knocks. When he reached deck level, Tyne began yelling for mercy. His voice was hopelessly muffled.

He was pulled across the deck to the rail.

Sweating, kicking feebly, he felt himself being lowered over the side. This is it, Leslie, he told himself in furious despair. He was swinging free. Then he felt the blessed hardness of a boat beneath him. The girl had put him into what seemed to be a rowing boat.

Tyne was still half-swooning with relief, when the girl landed beside him. The boat rocked gently, then shot away from the ketch. So it had a motor: but the motor was completely silent.

A momentary, irrelevant insight into the way Rosks got away with so much came to him. The average Sumatran is a very poor man. His horizon is of necessity bounded by economic need. The concept of world loyalty is not beyond him, but the chance to sell a fishing boat, or a knife, or a ketch, at a staggering profit is something which cannot be forgone.

To a considerable extent, the Rosks had found themselves on neutral ground. Power politics is a hobby the poor cannot afford. Absolute poverty, like absolute power, corrupts absolutely.

'I can help you in some way, Todpuddle,' Benda Ittai said, resting her hand on the sail imprisoning Tyne.

By now, the situation was so much beyond Tyne, and to hear her speak English was so reassuring, that he could only think to mumble through his sheet. 'My name's Tyne Leslie.'

'The others in my party do not know I speak Earthian,' she said. 'I have learnt it secretly from your telecasts.'

31

'There must be quite a bit about you they don't know,' he said. 'Let me out of this portable tomb! You really had me frightened back there, believe me.'

She cut away at the canvas with her sharp knife. She would only make a hole for his face, so that he lolled in the bows like a mummy, staring at her.

Benda Ittai was as nervous as a courting mole.

'Don't look at me as if I am a traitor to my race,' she said uneasily. 'It is not so.'

'That was not quite what I was thinking,' he replied, grinning involuntarily. 'But how do you come into the picture? What are you to do with Murray?'

'Never mind me. Never mind anything! All this business is too big for you. Just be content I do not let you drown. It is enough for one day.'

The sea was still lake-calm. The mist still hung patchily about. Benda was steering by compass, and in a minute a small island, crowned with the inevitable palms, waded out of the blankness towards them. The girl cut the engine, letting them drift in towards a strip of beach lying between two arms of vegetation.

'I shall leave you here and you can take your chance,' she said. 'When Budo Budda returns to the boat, I tell him my duty is performed. Here the water is shallow enough. I will cut your binding and you will wade ashore. No doubt that a passing boat will soon see you.'

'Look,' he said desperately, as she severed the cocoon of sail, 'I'm very grateful to you for saving my life, but please, *please*, what is all this about?'

'I tell you the business is too large for you. With that, please be content.'

'Benda, that sort of talk implies I'm too small for the business. That's bad for my complexes. You must tell me what's happening. How can this information Murray has be so vital that everyone is willing to commit murder to get it?'

She made him climb overboard before she would loosen his wrists, in case he pounced on her. He stood waist-deep in water. She tossed the knife to him. As he stooped to retrieve it, glittering like a fish under water, she called, 'Your Murray carries what you would name a microfilm. On this film is a complete record of the imminent invasion of Earth by an Alpha fleet of ships. Our ship which arrived here five years ago is not what you think it is; your people were misled. It is only a forward reconnaissance weapon, designed to make a preliminary survey for those who

32

are now coming to invade. Against the slaughter to come, you or I, whatever we feel, can do nothing. Already it is really too late. Good bye!'

Tyne stood in the sea helplessly, watching till she vanished into the golden mist.

IV

THE solar system progressed towards the unassailable summer star, Vega. The Earth-Moon system wobbled round the sun, host and parasite eternally hand-in-hand. The planet spun on its rocky, unimaginable axis. The ocean swilled for ever uneasily in their shallow beds. Tides of multifarious life twitched across the continents. On a small island a man sat and hacked at the casing of a coconut.

His watch told him that it was 4.20, local time. It would be dark in three hours. If the heat mist held till sunset his chances of being picked up today were negligible.

Tyne stood up, still chewing the last morsel of coconut flesh, and flung the empty case into the water. In a few minutes, it drifted ashore again. He fumed at his own helplessness. Without the sun, he could not even tell in which direction Sumatra lay. There, wherever it was, the fate of man was being decided. If World Government could get hold of that precious spool of microfilm, counter measures could effectively be taken. Stobart had spoken vaguely of 'information'; did he know the true value of what Murray was carrying? It seemed possible that Tyne was the only man in the world who knew just what tremendous stakes were in the balance.

Or did Murray know?

Murray had killed his friend and would betray his kind. What sort of a man was he?

'If ever I get my hands on him . . .' Tyne said.

He was determined that he would no longer be a pawn in the big game. As soon as possible, he would take the initiative.

Unknown forces had hitherto carried him round, much as the revolving equator did; from now on, he would move for himself.

Accordingly, he made a tour of the island on which he had been marooned. It was not much more than ten acres in extent, probably an outlying member of the Mentawai group. On its far side, overlooking a tumbled mass of rock which extended far into the sea, was a ruined fortification. Possibly it dated from the Java-Sumatra troubles of the mid-twentieth century.

The fortification consisted of two rooms. In the inner one, a table rotted and an iron chest rusted. Inside the chest lay a broken lantern, a spade and a pick. Mildewed shelving lined one wall of the place.

For the next few hours, Tyne was busy building his own defences. He was not going to be caught helpless again.

As he worked, his brain ran feverishly over what the alien girl had told him. He was simultaneously appalled at the naïveté of Earth in accepting as the simple truth the tale the Rosks had spun on arrival, and at the mendacity of Alpha II in thus taking advantage of man's generous impulses. Yet it was difficult to see how either side could have behaved differently. Earth had no reason to believe the Rosk ship was other than what it claimed to be. And if the Rosks were truly set on invasion, then from a military point of view their preliminary survey of Earth's physical and mental climate was indeed a sound one.

Exasperation saturated Tyne, as it so frequently had done in the old days round the U.N.C.'s shiny council tables. For these damnable oppositions, it seemed useless to blame the persons involved; rather, one had to curse the forces that made them what they were.

After he had been working for an hour, a light breeze rose; the mist cleared, the sun shone. Low clouds in the horizon marked the direction of Sumatra. Tyne's clothes dried off, his mescahale lighter functioned again. He built himself a bonfire, lit it, and worked by its flickering radiance when the sun went down.

At last his work completed, he flung himself down on the sand, overlooking the beach where Benda Ittai had left him. The lights of one or two atomic freighters showed in the distance, taking no notice of his beacon. He slept.

When he woke, it was to cold and cramp. A chill wind blew. The time was only 9.40. Low over the sea a segment of moon rose, cool and superb. And a fishing boat was heading towards the island.

35

Tyne was going to be rescued! At the sight of the reassuringly familiar shape of a local boat, he realised how much he had dreaded seeing Budo Budda's ketch instead. At once he was jubilant.

'Here! Here I am! Help!' he called in Malayan, jumping up and flinging fresh wood on to his fire. The fishing boat moved rapidly, and was already near enough for the hiss of its progress over the water to be heard.

The boat carried a dim light halfway up the mast. Three men sat in it. One of them cried out in answer as they collapsed the single sail. The boat nosed in, bumping against the sand.

On his way down to meet them, Tyne paused. These men were muffled like Arabs. And one of them – that was a weapon in his hand! Alarm seized him. He turned to run.

'Stand still, Tyne Leslie!'

Reluctantly, he stopped and turned. Of the two who had jumped from the boat, one had flung back his hood. In the moonlight, his shock of white hair was dazzling, like a cloud round his head. It was War Colonel Budo Budda. He was aiming his gun up the beach at Tyne.

They were not twenty yards apart, Budda and his fellow Rosk standing by the lapping sea, Tyne up the narrow beach, near the fringe of trees. It was a lovely night, so quiet you could hear your own flesh crawl.

'Is good of you to light a signal to guide us,' Budda said. 'We grew tired of searching little islands for you.'

At the words, Tyne realised that their finding him was no accident. His heart sank still further as he realised that there was only one source from which they could have learnt he was still alive. Without thinking, he blurted out, 'Where is Benda Ittai?'

Budda laughed. It sounded like a cough.

'We have her safe. She is a fool, but a dangerous one. She is a traitor. We long suspected it, and set a trap to catch her. We did not leave her alone on the boat with you, as we declared we would; secretly, a man was hidden to watch her. When she returned alone, having left you here, he confronted her and overpowered her.'

Whatever they had done to her, she had evidently not revealed where she had left him. That girl was a good one, Rosk or no Rosk. Tyne thought with compunction of her returning to the ketch, only to be jumped on. He remembered her nervousness; the memory seemed to come back to him like a fresh wind.

'You're too bloody clever, Budda!' he shouted. 'You'll die of it one day.'

'But not today,' Budda said. 'Come down here, Tyne. I want to know what the Ittai woman told you.'

So that was why they did not shoot him outright! They needed to find out if Benda had passed on anything they did not know.

Without answering, he turned and ran up the beach, pelting for the trees. At once he heard the sound of firing; the unmistakable high-pitched hiss of the Roskian service gun, a big .88 with semi-self-propelled slugs. Then he was among the trees and the undergrowth, black, hunched, reassuring, in the dark.

He began immediately to double over to the left, on a course that would bring him rapidly back to the sea without leaving the shelter of the trees. As he dodged along he looked frequently over his shoulder. Budda and companion were momentarily nonplussed; after the poor performance Tyne had made earlier in their hands, they probably had not expected him to show initiative. After holding a brief confab, they took a torch from the boat and commenced up the beach at a trot, calling his name.

By this time, Tyne had worked round to their flank. He crouched on a low cliff directly overlooking boat and beach. Groping in the undergrowth, he found three hefty stones.

At that moment, the two Rosks were running to the top of the beach. Tyne held his breath. They yelled together, their torch went spinning, they crashed into the trap he had prepared earlier on. To guard against eventualities, Tyne had used the spade he discovered to dig a deep trench in the sand across the path anyone heading inland would take. Covered with the rotted shelving from the old fortification, which in its turn was covered lightly with sand, it made a perfect trap. As the Rosks stepped on the concealed boards, they pitched through into the trench. Owing to the steep lie of the beach at this point, an avalanche of fine sand immediately poured upon them.

Tyne's advantage could be only temporary, a matter of seconds at best.

As the Rosk in the boat stood up to see what the trouble was, Tyne flung the first stone at him. The man was clearly outlined against bright water, and only a few yards away. The stone struck his arm. He turned, raising a .88. A chunk of rock the size of a man's foot caught him in the stomach.

Almost as he doubled up, Tyne was down the sandy cliff and on top of him. He sprang like a leopard, knocking the Rosk flat.

37

A clout over the head with another stone laid him out cold. Tyne pitched him unceremoniously out on to the wet sand, jumped out himself, and pushed the boat savagely out to sea. Flinging himself after it he climbed aboard and hoisted the sail. A bullet from the shore shattered the lamp on the mast. Tyne felt oil and glass spatter his flesh, he laughed.

Turning he saw two figures, black against the sand, climb out of his trap and run to the water. They fired again. The big bullets whined out to sea as Tyne dropped flat.

Rosks could swim like sharks. In their first year on earth, before the trouble began, they had entered the Olympic Games and won all the aquatic events with ease. No doubt they could swim as fast as a fishing boat moving in a light breeze.

Fumbling into the bottom of the boat, Tyne's steel left hand found the gun dropped by the Rosk he had overpowered. He grabbed it with a whispered word of thanks.

Budda and his companion were wading out, still firing and clutching their torch. They made perfect targets. Steadying his aim over the side of the boat, Tyne drew a bead on the War-Colonel. The wind was taking the sail now, making the boat dip as it left the lee of the island. He tried to synchronise his firing with the motion, ignoring a hissing missile that slashed through a plank not a foot from his face.

It was funny to be trying to kill someone on such a grand night . . . Now!

The Rosk weapon was superb. Recoil was non-existent. Across the level waters, not so many yards from the boat, Budda croaked once like a frog and pitched forward into the sea, carrying the torch with him.

'My God!' Tyne said. He said it again and again, as his boat gathered speed, dragging him over the moon-smeared waves. After the shock of killing came the exultation of it; he was almost frightened by the savage delight of his new mood. He could do anything. He could save the world.

The exultation quenched itself as he wondered where Budo Budda was now; whether anything of the Rosk survived apart from the body peering fixedly down into dark water. Then Tyne deliberately turned to face more practical matters.

* * *

Midnight was an hour and a half away. Time slid away from him like the wake of the boat. Murray had to be found before the

38

Rosks reached him – unless he had been found already. Obviously, the first thing to be done on reaching the mainland was for Tyne to report all he knew to Stobart, or to someone in authority. To think to continue a lone hunt for Murray was foolish: yet Tyne found himself longing to do just that, to confront the monster, to . . .

Yes, he wanted to kill the big, laconic space captain. Even – and it was shrinkingly he recognised the urge in himself – he wanted to feel that terrible exhilaration of killing for its own sake.

But another side of his nature merely wanted to solve the puzzle of Murray's disappearance and all that hung upon it. Merely! Tyne fumed to think he had been unconscious during those vital seconds in Area 101, of which Murray had given one account, Stobart another. The truth might lie in either or neither of them, and the truth might never be revealed. Truth was a primal force, almost like gravity; like gravity, it was always there, yet some people never even realised its presence.

Pocketing the .88 gun, Tyne steadied the high, stiff tiller. One of his earliest memories, half embedded in the silt of forgetting, was of himself in his pram and certainly not more than three years old. He was throwing a toy out of his pram. The toy fell to the ground. Every time he threw it, the fool thing went *down*. He tried with other toys, with his shoes, his hat, his blankets. They all went down. He still remembered the disappointment of it. Even today, he still hated that lack of choice.

Truth had the same inevitability about it; he just had to go on throwing facts overboard and it would eventually reveal itself to him. This time it was worth persevering: the future of Earth hung upon it.

At the moment, it seemed to him almost an abstract problem. He knew he should be hating the Rosks, the five thousand of them here, the millions of them mustering back on Alpha II. Yet the hate did not work; could that be merely because he knew one of them to be both brave and beautiful?

He switched his attention to sailing. The sail was cumbersome, the boat did not handle readily. It would probably, Tyne reflected, take him longer to get back from the island to Sumatra than the scout ships took from Sumatra to Luna. Progress was a fever from which many parts of the world were immune; a thousand centuries on, and paddy fields would still be cultivated by hand. For a race set on attaining their blessings in the life to come, material innovation may be a complete irrelevance. Tyne, consequently, was going where the wind blew.

But he was lucky. A south-east monsoon wind had him. In half an hour, the coast was in sight. In another hour, Tyne was steering in under the dark cliffs, looking for a place to scramble ashore. On a small, rocky promontory, two native huts sagged under their load of thatch; a yellow light burned in one of them. Running the boat ashore on sand and stones, Tyne climbed out and made for the dwellings.

Among the trees stood a small kampong. It smelt good: smoky and sweet. Tyne found an old man, smoking the last half-inch of a cheroot in the moonlight, who would lead him to a road. As they walked, Tyne learnt with relief that he was no more than a dozen miles south of Padang.

'Not an hour's walking from here,' the old man said, 'is a telephone in which you may speak to certain people at the capital. If you say to them to send a fast car a fast car will come.'

'Thanks for the suggestion. I'll certainly do as you say. Where-abouts is this phone? In a house or a shop?'

'No, the telephone is in the new sea water works, where sea water is turned into food.'

Tyne recognised this description; the old man was referring to the plankton plant at Semapang. He thanked him gratefully when they reached the road, asking him to accept the fishing boat as a present. Much delighted with this, the native in return produced some food wrapped in a palm leaf, which he insisted Tyne should have. Tyne thanked him and set off with a good heart. The folded leaf contained boiled rice, pleasantly spiced and with a few shreds of asswabi added. Tyne ate ravenously as he walked. Though the road was no more than a track, every rut in it lay clearly exposed in the moonlight. On either side stood the jungle, still as an English wood, forbidding as an English summer.

Fifty minutes passed before he gained the first sight of the plankton plant. By then, Tyne was feeling less fresh than he had done. The moon was inclined to hide behind accumulating cloud. Leaning against a tree, he paused to rest and consider. Thunder grumbled like thought above the treetops.

Mina, when Tyne questioned her in the Roxy, had said that Murray was coming here, to the plankton plant. The spy patrol captain could have only one reason for visiting this place. The plant was completely automated; at the most, it was peopled only by an odd engineer during the day and a guard at night. Murray must have chosen the spot as a hideout until he could make contact with his Rosk agent. On the face of it, it seemed a remote and unlikely spot to choose: but that in itself might be a good reason for choosing it.

Tyne's mind was made up. In his pocket was a Roskian .88 gun. He would hunt down Murray himself; if he was here, he would find him. There was a personal score to be settled with Murray. After that would be time enough to phone Stobart of the U.N.C.

Through the enamelled outlines of the trees, the bulk of the plankton plant loomed. It looked, in the wan moonlight, like an iceberg. And like an iceberg, much of its bulk lay below water, for it stood on the edge of the sea, its rear facing on to land, its massive front thrusting out into the Indian Ocean.

Every day, millions of tons of sea water were sucked into its great vats, to be regurgitated later, robbed of their plankton content. These minute organisms were filtered into tanks of nutrient solution, fed and fattened, before being passed over to the synthesising process, which turned them into compressed foodstuffs, highly nourishing if barely palatable. Such plants, established at intervals round the shores of the Indian Ocean and the China Seas, had done much to alleviate the semi-famine conditions hitherto prevailing in the more populous areas of the tropics.

Tyne approached the place cautiously.

Though he had never been here before, he found it all familiar, thanks to the publicity it enjoyed. He knew that the plant was almost impossible to break into. Where, then, would a hunted man hide? One answer seemed most likely: on the seaward façade.

There, numerous arches and buttresses over the submarine mouth of the plant would afford shelter from the elements – and from all but a personal, on-the-spot-search.

Now Tyne was going to make that search.

He slid round a deserted car park. Clouds drifted over the moon; he was happy to take advantage of them. At the end of the park was a high wall. Over the wall was a narrow passage, and then the main building, rising sheer. Carrying an empty oil drum across to the wall, Tyne stood on it, crouched, jumped upwards. Clawing desperately, he pulled himself on top of the wall. He crouched and listened. Nothing. Only the murmur of the sea, the stammering call of a night bird.

The impossibility of getting on to the building now dawned on him. The white walls rose a hundred and fifty feet above him, stretching away unbrokenly on either side, and punctuated only

41

by a dark streak some yards away. Keeping his head down, Tyne wormed along the top of the wall; the dark streak resolved itself into a steel ladder, starting some fourteen feet above the ground and going right up to the roof.

Tyne, getting opposite to it, stood up on the wall and jumped forward, across the passage below. Seizing the rungs with both hands, he got a foothold. His steel hand was nearly wrenched from its socket with the sudden exertion; he clung there motionless until the pain in his arm had subsided. The darkness grew thicker and thicker while he waited. Thunder rumbled overhead. Then he began the upward climb.

Even as he started, the rain began. Tyne heard it swishing through the jungle towards him. Next moment it hit him as if trying to squash him against the wall. He wondered grimly how long it was since he had last been completely dry and continued to climb.

Once on the roof, he squatted and peered about him, trying to see through the wet darkness. Raincloud now obscured the moon. To his right, he saw tall ventilation stacks and heard the rain drumming against them. He was cursing, half-aloud. He was cursing the whole universe, suns and moons and planets but expecially planets, for harbouring freak phenomena like life and weather.

Advancing on hands and knees, he made for the seaward side. One last ridge to crawl up, one last ridge to slither periously down, and he crouched on the top of the façade of the building. Below him were the arches and cavities in which he expected to find Murray. Below that, irritable now, lay the sea.

He could dimly see it, needled unceasingly by the downpour, sucking and slumping against the plant. Immediately below him was a patch of relatively calm water. This lay inside the plankton mesh, a vast perforated screen which ensured that nothing larger than a small shrimp would be sucked into the plant's internal processes. On the other side of the mesh, spray fountained.

In the noise about him, Tyne had lost the need for concealment. He stood up now and shouted, cupping his hands round his mouth.

'Murray!'

The cry was washed away at once into the gutters of soundlessness. He did not shout again.

With water streaming down his face, Tyne dropped on to hands and knees, to begin a crawl along the leading parapet, looking for another inspection ladder that would enable him to get down the façade.

He found one. Grinning to himself with satisfaction, he swung his legs over the edge of the drop. As he took his first foothold, a shot rang out.

Tyne froze. He crouched with his head against the streaming concrete, body tensed against pain. It was impossible to tell where the shot had come from, from above or from below. For the space of ten unendurable seconds, he lay rigid. Then he slithered down the ladder as fast as he could go, heedless of the pain in his good hand and wrist. The wind buffeted him as he went.

No more shots sounded. But in the dark, someone was trailing him.

Tyne climbed off the ladder on to a narrow catwalk. Here was shelter. The architects responsible for the elaborate artificiality of this seaward façade had arched off this layer of it with a row of small, blind tunnels. If Murray was anywhere in the vicinity, the chances were that he would be here. As Tyne entered the first arch, a startled seabird clattered past his face, squawking. He stood quite still until his heart stopped jumping.

Then he began to move from one arch to the next, fumbling, looking for Murray. It was a nerve-racking business. Underfoot, a slippery mess of bird droppings made the going doubly perilous.

He had reached the third arch along when a watery moon slid through for a moment. Glancing back over his shoulder, Tyne saw a figure climbing down the steps he had just left. Man or Rosk? And if man: was it Murray? Acting hurriedly but indecisively, Tyne swung round to face his pursuer. His foot slid across the slippery concrete, went over the edge.

Before he could save himself, Tyne had fallen from the catwalk. For an instant, his ten fingers, five steel, five painfully flesh, scraped safety; then he was dropping freely, plunging down towards the sea.

Dark water slammed up to meet him. He hit it shoulder first and went under. As he came up gasping, he saw he was inside the plankton mesh.

Someone seemed to be calling from a long way off. The rain beat down like a solid thing, raising slashes from the sea, so that the surface was impossible to define. Tyne choked down water as he swam for the wall.

Then over all the rest of the noise came a new one. It was low and continuous, the roar of a superhumanly angry bull. Tyne felt his legs caught, his progress halted, as if the sound itself had hold of him. He was being drawn underwater. Fighting, shouting, he realised what was happening. The plant's subterranean intake gates had opened. He was inside the screen. He was going to be turned into plankton juice.

Somewhere below him, sluices swung wide. The man was dragged under, over and over, swept into the throat of the great plant, helpless as a leaf in a storm. The last shreds of light and air were torn from his world.

V

THE swamping pounding liquid registered on his tousled sense as sound: sound roaring him to death.

In the blundering blackness before Tyne's eyes, pictures squirmed like worms, sharing his agony. They were images of his past life bubbling up, scum-like, to the surface of his drowning brain. Incidents from his personal history returned to him, enfolding him as if to protect him from present pain. Then they were gone.

The bubble of the past had burst. His head was above water again. Exhaustedly, gulping down air, Tyne paddled to keep afloat in the racing water. Faint, reflected lights rode on the flood round him. He was somewhere inside the huge, automated plant, which was dimly lit by multicoloured guidelights here and there. The factory was cybernetically controlled, tenanted by robot devices. No one would save him if he could not save himself.

In his relief at finding his head above water, Tyne did not for a minute realise the grimness of his new predicament. He was simply content to float at the top of a rising tide of water, breathing and snorting painfully. Beyond thick glass, he could see the interior of the plant, where a shadowy file of processing tanks, moving by jerks, slowly revolved vats of jelly; endless pipes and presses marched into the background. He could see too, negligently, successive floors of the edifice sink from his gaze as the water lifted him up and up.

His mind snapped back into something like its normal degree of awareness. Searchingly, Tyne looked about. He had come up through the bottom of, and was now imprisoned in, a great glass tube with a diameter of some fifteen feet, standing a full six stories high.

Peering through the glass in sudden agitation, Tyne saw other giant tubes ranged alongside his, like the pipes of some overblown organ. The tubes stretched from base to roof of the plant, through all floors, and were filling rapidly with the incoming sea water.

Tyne looked up. The ceiling was growing closer. The tube was filling right up to the top.

This was inevitable. He knew immediately where he was. These entry tubes took each intake of water. When they were filled, great filter plungers came down from the top like slow pistons, filtering through the sea water, compressing plankton to the bottom of the tube; and not only plankton, but any other solid which happened to be there. Mercifully, Tyne Leslie would be dead by drowning before he was crushed against the bottom.

Between the turbulent water surface and the underside of the plunger, only some nine feet remained; the distance was decreasingly rapidly.

Groaning, treading water, Tyne felt in his trouser pocket. The Rosk .88 was still there. Tearing it free, Tyne lifted it above the surface of the water.

Six feet left between him and the plunger.

He prayed that a man who had once told him that these weapons were unaffected by water had spoken the truth. Shaking it, he turned over on to his back, floated, aimed at the glass imprisoning him.

Five feet of air above him.

He squeezed the trigger. As always with this incredible weapon, there was no recoil. The big slug shattered the tube up, down and sideways, converting it in a flash into a multitude of glass shards, a foot thick and some of them a couple of stories long. Tyne was swept at this fearsome barrier by the weight of released water.

It carried him right out into the factory. For a moment, a great gulf extending down into the bowels of the plant hung below him. Then he snatched at and clung to a balcony railing. His arms creaked at their sockets but he clung there. As though for an age, Tyne hung on; as though for an age, water and glass cascaded past him, a waterfall containing death. With a great effort he climbed over the rail to safety, hardly realising himself alive.

Another sound roused him, a sound easy to identify: a siren

was wailing; directly he punctured the big tube, an automatic alarm had gone off.

To be caught in here would mean the end of everything. Forfeiting his freedom might mean losing the last chance of finding Murray, even the last chance of passing the vital information gained from Benda Ittai on to the proper authorities. Tyne got up, dripping, pushing the wet hair back from his eyes. He was on a catwalk; a couple of feet away, crates of processed plankton, now disguised as steaks and pastes and spreads, moved briskly on a conveyor belt. And rapid footsteps sounded near at hand.

The dark was penetrated by widely spaced lights, some red, some orange, some blue. Peering through the gravy blackness in which swabs of light swam, Tyne saw a figure running round the catwalk towards him. Two figures! Whoever had pursued him outside, had managed to follow him into here. Someone with keys to the place.

'Leslie! Tyne Leslie!' a voice called.

It was magnified, distorted, made metallic, by the acoustics of the building; Tyne did not think he would have recognised it, even in more favourable circumstances. With sudden fear, he felt convinced that the Rosks were after him. He jumped on to the conveyor belt.

He slipped, knocking a crate off the other side; the belt was travelling considerably faster than he had estimated. In some alarm, Tyne knelt up, staring back to see where his pursuer was. At that moment, he himself was borne under an orange light. Cursing lest he had given himself away, Tyne turned to see where he was being carried.

A low entrance loomed just ahead.

Involuntarily, Tyne shouted with alarm. He ducked. At once, impenetrable darkness swallowed him. He was in a tunnel. His elbow hissed against a moving side wall, and he tucked it in hastily. He dared not raise his head. There was nothing to be done but crouch between crates.

The conveyor emerged suddenly into a packing bay. A robot loader under a bright light was pushing the crates shut when they filled. That was not for Tyne. He rolled off the belt just before the robot got to him.

There was no time to choose how he was going to drop. He fell painfully flat on the floor, picking himself up slowly and wearily. His watch told him that it was nearly 3.30 a.m. He should be in bed and asleep. He ached all over.

Even as he got to his feet, the conveyor exit ejected his two pursuers. They, apparently, knew better than Tyne what to expect; as they catapulted into the packing room, they jumped clear one after the other, landing nimbly on their feet. Before Tyne could make up his mind to move, they had collared him.

'Come on, Leslie; let's get you out of here,' one of them said, holding tightly on to his arm.

They were masked.

Tyne could see nothing of their faces beyond their forehead and their eyes, which looked at him over the top of knotted handkerchiefs.

'Who are you?' he asked feebly. 'Why the yashmak effect?'

'Explanation later,' one of the men said. 'Let's concentrate on getting you out of this building before half Padang arrives to investigate that alarm.'

The siren was still shrilling as the men led Tyne down a couple of floors, unlocked a door with a special key, and pushed him into the open. At an awkward jog trot, they hurried down a slope, their way intermittently lit by lightning. Although rain still fell, its force was hesitant now; the storm had worn itself out. Water gurgled down into storm drains beside their path.

A door stood at the end of the passage. The burlier of the two men, evidently the one in authority, produced another key, unlocked the door and flung it open.

They emerged behind an almost deserted car park, not far from the point at which Tyne had first tackled the building. Trotting across the puddle-strewn ground, they ran to an ancient model of a Moeweg, a German atomicar. Burly flung himself into the driver's seat as the others bundled into the back. He jerked the dipstick and they were moving at once.

As they accelerated past the front of the plant, the first car to answer the alarm call arrived from the opposite direction. It had a searchlight mounted on the roof; it was a police car. As the old Moeweg dashed by, a uniformed man leant out of the police car and bellowed to them to stop. Burly accelerated.

'Damn it, they'll have our number,' he said over his shoulder, to the man beside Tyne. 'We'll meet trouble as sure as eggs. I'm going to turn off before we hit traffic; this is no time to play questions and answers with a bunch of local cops.'

A fire engine dashed past them. A helicopter thundered overhead. Bright headlights through the trees indicated a stream of traffic heading round a bend for the scene of the alarm. Burly wrenched the dip; they slewed across the road and squealed into a narrow lane leading into jungle.

The lane had been intended for nothing bigger than a cowcart. Foliage whapped and smacked against the windows as the car lunged forward.

'It's crazy!' Tyne thought, 'all absolutely crazy!' He had time to wonder about the respect he had held for men of action. He had seen them as people at the equator of life, in the hottest spots, going round the fastest; he saw now it was true only in a limited sense. These people merely went in circles. One minute they were hunters, the next hunted. They made decisions rapidly, yet those decisions seemed based less on a rational understanding and interpretation of their opponent's motives than on a desire to keep hopping continually in an immense, indeterminate game.

A game! That was the secret of it all! These men of action could enter a contest involving life and death only because once they had plunged in, the stakes became unreal. This was chess, played with adrenalin instead of the intellect. They had got beyond the ordinary rules of conduct.

The terrible thing was, Tyne found, that although he now saw this clearly enough, he too was caught in the game – voluntarily. World events had become too grave to be treated seriously. One could escape from all their implications by sinking into this manic sub-world of action, where blood and bluff ruled. By the same token, he saw the pendulum which ruled the sub-world sliding back in his favour. These men had caught Tyne when he was unprepared; now that he was in their hands, he could be relaxed but alert; in a sense, he had no care; they had the worries. When this pressure grew to a certain pitch, they would become in their turn unprepared – and he would elude them. It was inevitable, just a rule in the crazy game. After that, of course, the big pendulum would swing the other way again.

'This is far enough,' Burly said, when the Moeweg had rocked and staggered some hundreds of yards into the jungle. The man beside Tyne never uttered a word.

The car stopped, and with an effort Tyne brought his attention back to the present. His mind had been busily elaborating his theory – even giving it some such half-jocular title as Leslie's Principle of Reciprocal Action, or the Compensatory Theory of Irresponsible Activity (Leslie's Effect) – with the same attention it had once devoted to preliminary drafts of official memoranda.

Burly flicked off the headlights, so that only the dash light illuminated them. Outside, the rain had stopped, though the foliage overhead still dripped meditatively on to the car roof. It was 4.15, a numb, light-headed time of night.

'All right,' Tyne said, 'now suppose you tell me who you are, what you're doing, and why you think you're doing it?'

Removing the cloth which had covered the lower part of his face, Burly turned in his seat to look at Tyne.

'First of all,' he said, in a gentle, educated voice, 'we ought to apologise for virtually kidnapping you like this, Mr Leslie. Time pressed, and we had no alternative. I ought perhaps to add – forgive me – that none of this would have been necessary if you had waited for us to explain when we caught you up on the façade of the plankton plant. Your dive into the sea was spectacular, but unnecessary.'

'I didn't dive,' Tyne said, wryly. 'I slipped.'

Abruptly, Burly burst into laughter. Tyne found himself joining in. The tension eased considerably. The masked man beside Tyne never moved.

'This is the situation,' Burly said. 'My name, by the way, is Dickens – Charles Dickens. No relation, of course. I am working with the man you know as Stobart, the U.N.C. agent; his second-in-command, as it were. You have been missing now for some hours, and we frankly were worried. You see, your role in this affair is an ambiguous one; we naturally like to know where you are.'

'Naturally. What made you look for me at the plankton plant?' Tyne inquired. 'Or shouldn't I ask?'

'We weren't looking for you,' Dickens said. 'We just happened to be searching the place at the time you came along. Like you, we were hoping to find Murray Mumford there.'

'How did you know I was still looking for Murray?'

'You called his name, remember? For another thing, Mina, Murray's woman, told you to go there. *She* told you Murray had said he would be at the plankton plant.'

Tyne suddenly fell silent. Dickens' words brought back a vital memory to him, something that he had recalled during those terrible moments of drowning in the plant. The memory gave him the key to Murray's whereabouts; he must get away from Dickens and his silent partner as soon as he had as much information as possible from them. Dragging his mind back to the present, he asked, 'How did you find out about Mina, Dickens?'

'Stobart found out. He questioned her after you'd left him. We've not been sitting down doing nothing.'

'Don't talk to me about Stobart. There's a man who should learn a few manners before he mixes with people.'

'Stobart is something of a psychologist,' Dickens said. 'He deliberately made his advice to you to stop looking for Murray so unpalatable that you would ignore it.'

Tyne smiled to himself. These boys thought they had all the answers. What they did not know was that he had, in fact, already stopped looking for Murray when the Rosk picked him up in the taxi. Stobart could stuff that up his psychology.

'So Stobart wanted me as a stooge,' he said. 'Why?'

'You were just one of his impromptu ideas. The Rosks had him cornered in the Roxy when you arrived. You were a diversion to draw them away. Actually, you were doubly useful. After the Rosks had taken you out to their ketch –'

'What!' Tyne exploded. Suddenly he was furiously angry. The silent man beside him placed a restraining hand on his arm, but Tyne knocked it off with his steel fist. 'You mean you people know about that ketch? Yet you let it stay there? You let me be tortured – well, I was nearly tortured there. You let that thug of Ap II Dowl's, Budo Budda, come and go there as he pleased? And all the time you *knew* about the ketch and could have blown it out of the water? Isn't it infringing the interplanetary agreement by being there?'

'Don't get excited. We didn't know you were taken to the ship; the Rosks picked you up too quickly for that – you weren't half awake, Leslie! We were waiting for big game; Ap II Dowl is to visit that ketch in the early hours of this morning. By now, in fact, we should have trapped him there. If we can get him in the bag, many of Earth's troubles will be over.'

'You don't know how many troubles she's got,' Tyne said grimly. 'She is about to be attacked by an Alpha II invasion fleet. That's the cheering news Murray carries round with him.'

'We know.'

'You know! How do you know?'

'We have means, Mr Leslie; leave it at that.'

As Dickens spoke, a buzzer sounded. A radio telephone was installed on the Moeweg's dashboard, Dickens picked it up, listened, spoke into it in a low voice; Tyne caught his own name being mentioned.

'Can't you ever think of a word to say?' he asked the man sitting next to him. The other shrugged his shoulders and made no answer.

Suddenly Dickens thrust the phone down and swore luridly.

He cursed with vigour and a vinegary wit, making it as obscene as possible. It was a startling display, coming from him.

'Leslie, you've properly buggered things up,' he said, swinging round in the car seat. 'That was Stobart calling. He says you were marooned on a small island called Achin Itu until about ten o'clock this evening – that is, yesterday evening. They found your monogrammed mecahale lighter on the beach. Is that a fact?'

'I'd like that lighter back; it cost me fifty chips. Tell Stobart, will you?'

'Listen, Leslie, you shot up that Rosk Colonel, Budda. Do you know what you've done? You scared Ap II Dowl away! When he got wind of Budda's death, he stayed tight in the base. Our fellows raided the ketch an hour back, while you were playing tag over the plankton plant, and got nothing but a lot of useless information.'

'Don't blame me, Dickens. Call it one of my impromptu ideas, eh? Any time one of Stobart's plans go wrong, give me the word; I find I get a thrill out of hearing about it.'

'You're coming back to Padang with me, Leslie, right away. We're going to lock you up until you learn not to make a nuisance of yourself.'

'Oh, no you don't!' Tyne said, half-getting out of his seat. Something hard pressed against his side. He looked down. The silent partner was digging in with a revolver, his eyes unwavering above the handkerchief. Dickens switched the car headlights on again as Tyne sat back helplessly in his seat.

'That's right, relax,' Dickens said. 'From now on, you're living at the government's expense.'

'But I've got a hunch about finding Murray,' Tyne said. 'I swear to you, Dickens, I may be able to go straight to him. You still want him, don't you?'

'We'd trade in the U.N.C. Building for him,' Dickens said quietly, starting the engine. 'But things are too complex for you, feller. There's no room outside for amateurs just at present; you've done enough damage. Here's another thing you didn't know. Have you paused to wonder why the Rosks couldn't slip a roll of microfilm smaller than your little finger from Luna to Earth themselves? There's a reason why they got Murray to carry it. It's stolen from the Rosks.'

'You mean the Rosks stole the film from the Rosks?'

'Yes; that's what I said and what I mean. Ever heard of the Roskian peace faction, the RPF, led by Tawdell Co Barr? They're a small and semi-illegal organisation of Rosks ranged against Ap II Dowl and pledged to work for peace with Earthmen. Their numbers are few. In Luna Area 101 there can't be more than a handful of them. But they managed to get their hands on this film, and of course they want it to reach the main body of RPF in the Sumatran base here. I fancy it'll be used for propaganda purposes, to show the Rosks what a blood-thirsty maniac Dowl is.

'I tell you this so that you can see why the situation is too complex for you; it comes in layers, like an onion.'

Even as he spoke, Dickens was wrestling with the car. The wheels spun in mud but did not move. While they waited here for the alarm on the main road to die down, the heavy vehicle had sunk into the soft track. Tyne scarcely noticed what was happening as he mulled over what Dickens had told him. It threw new light on at least one Rosk: the girl, Benda Ittai, who had saved his life.

'Have you ever heard of Benda Ittai?' Tyne asked. Speaking her name aloud filled him with an unexpected pleasure.

'We're bogged down, damn it,' Dickens said. 'Oh, how I love Sumatra! Benda Ittai is evidently one of the RPF. Stobart's men found her on the ketch when they raided it. The Rosks were about to put her to death. Under the circumstances, our men found it best to let her go free; I tell you, Stobart has a soft heart – I'd have locked her up. Damn this filthy, soggy country! I can understand how they get volunteers for lunar duty. Yes, if I had my way, I'd clap her in prison; I'd clap all of you – look, I'm getting out to put something under the wheels. Leslie, if you try to escape, my friend will shoot you in the leg. It's painful. Do by all means try it and see.'

He climbed out, leaving his door swinging open. His feet squelched in the wet grass, and he steadied himself against the Moeweg's bonnet.

Tyne's heart thudded. He wondered if he stood a chance of overpowering the fellow beside him. Dickens was visible through the windscreen, bathed in bright light which only emphasised the sad waiting darkness of the forest on either side. The agent had produced a small sheath knife and was hacking at the thick fronds of a bush, throwing them under the car's front wheels.

Then something else was moving out there. It came swishing in from the treetops with a vibrant humming. Bushes and twigs writhed and cringed; everything seemed to turn alive at its approach.

Dickens straightened and saw it. Beautifully in control of himself, he dropped the foliage he had cut and reached for a holstered gun without a second's pause. As his hand came up, he fired two shots at the thing, then turned and leapt into the Moeweg, slamming the door shut behind him. Furiously, he made a fresh attempt to extricate the car from the mud. The flying thing charged at them, bowling in from the bending darkness.

'What is it? What the devil is it?' Tyne asked, severely rattled. He began to sweat. His ears jarred with the noise the thing made.

'It's a Rosk fly-spy,' Dickens said, without turning his head. 'Sort of flying eye. Televises reports of all it sees back to Rosk base. I've seen a captured one back at H.Q. They're unarmed but definitely not harmless. Mind it doesn't – ah!'

They jerked forward a foot then fell back again, their wheels failing to grip. The fly-spy hovered then dropped almost to ground level. Tyne saw it clearly now. It was a fat disc perhaps five feet in diameter and two feet six at its greatest width. Lenses of varying size studded its rim and under surface. An inset search-light swivelled a blinding beam of light at them.

Rotors probably mounted on a gyroscope powered the machine. They set up the humming note making the bushes in their vicinity move uneasily as if trying to escape observation. The rotors were set inside the disc protected by fine mesh from possible damage.

It moved forward suddenly. Even as Dickens instinctively ducked the fly-spy struck their windscreen, shattering it into tiny fragments. Dickens swore ripely.

'The Rosk base isn't far from here!' he shouted. 'Just a few miles through the jungle. If this thing has identified us it may be planning to wreck the car – to hold us up till a Rosk patrol can get at us. Cover your face up Leslie – don't let it see who you are!'

The fly-spy had lifted. It hovered somewhere above the vehicle. They couldn't see it, but they could hear it, the venomous note of a hornet, amplified. All the leaves near the car waved furiously, enduring their own private storm. Tyne was tying a handkerchief round his face when Dickens flung the engine into reverse. Bucking wildly, the old Moeweg heaved itself out of the pit it had gouged for itself. At once the fly-spy returned to the attack. With a slicing movement, it sped down and struck one of the rear side windows. It did not retreat, just stayed there pushing, huge through the shattered glass, its lens seeming to sparkle with malice. The car lurched, the coach-work crumpled.

The silent agent scrambled up on to the seat, taking pot shots through the broken window. His forehead was grey and patchy above his mask.

'Aim at its rotors through the mesh!' Dickens bellowed. 'That's the only way you'll knock it out!'

They were speeding recklessly backwards down the jungle track. Dickens drove looking over his shoulder, dipstick in one hand, gun in the other.

'That thing can squash you if you try to run for it.' he said. 'Squash you flat against the ground.'

'I wasn't planning to jump out,' Tyne replied. He had just been planning to jump out.

As he spoke, the silent man flung open his door, hanging out to get a better shot into the middle of the fly-spy's works. The thing reared up immediately into the branches overhead – and crashed down into one of the back wheels. The Moewog skidded sideways into the bushes and stopped, engine bellowing uselessly.

Tyne hardly paused to think. He knew they were trapped now. This thing could batter the car apart if it was so directed.

The dumb agent had been pitched on to the ground by the skid. Leaping through the open door, Tyne jumped on to him, snatched his gun and lunged into the undergrowth. He dived into the bushes recklessly, doubled up, doing anything to get away. Moving on hands and knees, he charged forward, heedless of any cuts or tears he sustained. Shots sounded behind him; he did not know if Dickens was firing at him or the fly-spy.

He travelled fast. He tumbled into a little overgrown stream and was out in a flash. The faintest light, perhaps the first light of dawn, aided him.

He knew what to do. He was heading for a belt of thick trees with low branches. The fly-spy had severe limitations, for all its power. Dense foliage would stop it.

Tyne was on his feet now, running doubled up. He no longer knew which way he was running. That deep, determined humming sounded behind him. A light flickered and swam among the leaves, as the searchlight sought him out. The leaves writhed. Where were the damned trees?

Blowing hard, he pounded through chest-high vegetation. It seemed endless.

Now he bounded down a bushy slope, plunged into a line of trees, tore himself free of brambles. When he tripped a minute later, he could hardly get up. Looking wearily above his head, he saw against the dark sky a protecting network of branches.

The smaller branches waved in an artificial wind.

Panting, Tyne lay there like a trapped animal.

All he could do, he had done. He hadn't imagined it would come after him; he had thought it would stay by the car and the two U.N.C. agents. But . . . if its transmissions back to Rosk base had caused him to be identified there as the Earthman to whom Benda Ittai had spoken, then there was good reason for his being the quarry.

The leaves and grasses trembled about him. The resonant hum filled his ears. Jumping up like a frightened stag, Tyne flung himself into one of the trees. Pulling himself up, he hauled himself ten, fifteen feet above ground, hugging the trunk among a welter of stout, out-thrusting branches.

Seeing was better now. First light drifted like sludge through the trees. The slope he had run down lay in one direction, a fast river in the other. On the other side of the river lay what looked like a track.

The fly-spy had seen him. It swooped in low, cutting above the ground, its light probing. It could not rise to him because of the branches; they shielded him as he had hoped. Instead, the machine nuzzled lightly against the tree bole. For the first time, looking down on it, Tyne saw its big fans, revolving in a whirl behind protective gratings. He fired at them with the agent's gun. His arm shook, the shot went wild.

The machine backed away and butted the tree. Then it circled out, seeking another way to get at him. Almost at the same time, Tyne became aware of Dickens, running down the slope. Following the fly-spy's noise, the agent had followed Tyne.

Branches cracked. The fly-spy was pushing through twigs and light branches on a level with Tyne. Tyne slid round the other side of the trunk. If he could only hold out till full daylight, this thing would be bound to go home or else risk detection. He squinted down below but Dickens had disappeared.

Again he changed position, to keep the tree's girth between himself and the machine. This meant slipping down to a lower branch. He must beware of being forced all the way down; on the ground he was defenceless. The thing droned angrily, like an immense spinning top, pushing persistently through a maze of twigs. It worked to one side; again Tyne worked away from it.

Suddenly there was a shout, and the sound of shoes kicking steel.

Tyne looked round the tree, peering out like a scared squirrel. Dickens had jumped or fallen on to the fly-spy! The agent had climbed the next tree and then launched himself, or dropped outwards. Now he sprawled on top of the disc, fighting to get a grasp of it.

'Dickens!' Tyne yelled.

The agent slithered over the rocking surface of the fly-spy. His legs dangled, kicking wildly in air. Then he caught a finger hold in the machine's central mesh and drew himself into a more secure position. As the fly-spy rocked among the branches, he pulled his gun out, aiming it at the rotor blades.

All this had obviously taken the Rosks who controlled the big disc completely by surprise. It just drifted where it was, helplessly. Then it moved. Its pervasive note changing pitch, it shot up like an express lift.

Dickens was knocked flat by a bough. Partially stunned, he slithered once more over the side, and his gun went flying – clatter-clattering all the way from branch to branch down to the ground.

'Jump, Dickens, for God's sake!' Tyne shouted.

It was doubtful if the agent heard a word of it. He was carried up through the foliage, hanging on grimly, head half-buried in his arms. The last leaves swished by, and the fly-spy was out in the open, climbing slowly.

Heedlessly, Tyne jumped from the tree to sprawl full length in a flowering bush. Picking himself up, he broke from the trees, running along below the fly-spy, shouting incoherently. He dared not fire in case he hit Dickens.

In the vapid early morning light, the disc was clearly visible thirty feet up, heading fast on an unswerving course that would, Tyne guessed, take it back to Sumatran base, where the Rosks awaited it. Dickens had evidently had the same thought. He knelt on top of the thing, wrenching at the screens on its upper surface. In a moment, he had unlatched a segment of screen, a wedge-shaped bit that left the rotors revolving nakedly underneath.

He wrenched his shoe off and flung it into the rotors.

At once the dynamic hum changed into a violent knocking. From the knocking grew the mirthless squeal of metal breaking up. With a few staccato grinding sounds, the fly-spy began to fall, canting sharply.

Tyne was still running when it crashed into the river he had noticed earlier, bearing its passenger with it. They disappeared with a splash and did not come up again.

VI

Iᴛ was 9.15 in the morning.

Tyne Leslie sat at the back of a Chinese coffee shop, eating durian off a cracked plate. His cheeks were smooth, his head was clear; he had been to a nappi wallah who had shaved him and massaged his head and shoulders. When he had finally plodded into Padang, ninety minutes ago, after a fruitless search along the river bank for Dickens, he had felt half-dead. Now he was, after a shave, the massage and breakfast, alive again, alert, planning ahead, casting little feelers of worry into the future.

Already he had written a note to Under-Secretary Grierson, a second secretary to whose under-secretary Tyne had been, outlining that threat of invasion to Earth. That note had been delivered to the British Diplomatic Mission building, and would be before the Under-Secretary himself within an hour. How long it would be before any action was taken on it was another matter.

Meanwhile time grew short. Murray had been at large in Padang for twenty-four hours. If the Roskian RPF agent had been unable to reach Murray, it would be because he had been dogged by his own people, the Rosks faithful to Ap II Dowl. Undoubtedly though, the parties interested in finding Murray were closing in: RPF, Dowl's men, the U.N.C., and possibly – undoubtedly, if they had wind of the affair – various nationally interested Earth groups. And Tyne.

And Tyne. He had told Dickens he was prepared to go straight to Murray. It was the truth. By a paradox, he could have done as much yesterday, before Stobart spoke to him.

The truth had lain, as so often happens, inside him, waiting for the ripe moment to reveal itself.

When Tyne questioned Mina in the Roxy foyer, she said that Murray had announced he was going to the plankton plant. She had assumed – and Tyne had unthinkingly accepted her assumption – that Murray meant the plant at Semapang, where he had nearly drowned himself. When Stobart had questioned the girl later, he had got the same answer; that was why Tyne and Dickens had met at the building.

But Murray had meant something quite different when he spoke of the plankton plant.

In those terrible seconds when Tyne was dragged drowning through the submarine intakes at Semapang, scenes from his past life had bubbled through his mind. One scene had been of Murray, Allan Cunliffe and himself breakfasting at the Merdeka Hotel after a heavy night. While he and Allan sat drinking coffee, Murray tucked in to a large breakfast, complaining all the time about the badness of the food. 'It's always synthetic at the Merdeka,' he said. 'Doesn't matter what the food resembles, it's really plankton underneath. As the Americans say, it's a plant. A plankton plant! I tell you dreary-looking couple of so-and-sos, we live in a plankton plant. Before you know it, the management will be offering us plankton women . . . '.

The comments had stuck. From then on, the three of them had occasionally referred to the Merdeka as 'the plankton plant'; it had been a private joke between them, until they tired of it.

All of this had run through Tyne's drowning mind. He knew now that to find Murray he had to go to the Merdeka again; that was the place Murray had been referring to. Mina had been misled; so had Stobart; naturally enough, for they had never heard the old private joke. Tyne had been once, fruitlessly, to the Merdeka; today, he was going to ask the right questions of the right people.

Settling his bill, he left the cafe. He had already purchased a spare clip of ammunition for the stolen gun in his pocket. Now he moved through side streets, warily, alert for danger. A protest march of the displaced, complete with drums and banners ('ROSKS LEAVE OUR WORLD TO PEACE'. 'WORLD POWERS ARE DUPES OF ALIENS'. 'SUMATRA HAS BEEN SACRIFICED!'), acted as convenient cover as Tyne slipped into the foyer of the hotel.

The familiarity, at once welcome and repugnant, of the place assailed him like a pervasive fog. At this hour, before Padang's political life, with its endless conferences and discussions, was under way, the lounge was full of the sort of men Tyne had been: restless, wretched (but smiling) men who continually manoeuvred, but never manoeuvred boldly enough. Tyne skirted them, feeling as alien to them as a Rosk might have done.

He went through the building into the rear courtyard, where two very ancient Chinese ladies were combing each other's hair in the sunshine.

'Have you seen Amir, please?' Tyne asked.

'He is at the warehouse, checking the rations.'

The 'warehouse' was a crude brick shed beyond the courtyard, tucked between other buildings and conveniently facing a small back lane. Outside it stood a little delivery van, labelled in Malayan, Chinese and English, 'Semapang Plankton Processed Foodstuffs.' The Merdeka was getting its daily quota of nourishment.

As Tyne approached, a uniformed driver emerged from the warehouse, climbed into the van and drove off. Tyne went stealthily to the warehouse door. Amir was there alone, left arm in a sling, leaning over a box checking delivery notes. Tyne entered, closing the door behind him.

Amir had been something of a friend of Allan's and Tyne's. Now there was only fear on his dark, intelligent face as he looked up and recognised his visitor.

'What have you done to your arm, Amir?'

'I thought you were dead, Mr Leslie!'

'Who told you that?'

'You should not be here! It is dangerous here, Mr Leslie! The Merdeka is always being watched. Please go away at once. For everyone's safety, go away!'

His agitation was painful to watch. Tyne took his good arm and said: 'Listen, Amir, if you know there is danger, you must know something of what is happening. The lives of everyone on Earth are threatened. I have to find Murray Mumford at once. At once! Do you know where he is?'

To his surprise and embarrassment, the young Sumatran began to weep. He made no noise or fuss about it; the tears rolled down his cheeks and fell on to the clean floor. He put up a hand to cover his eyes.

'So much trouble has been caused my country by other countries. Soon I shall join the Displaced. When our numbers are big enough, we shall force all foreigners to leave our land.'

'And the Rosks,' Tyne added.

60

'*All foreigners.* Do you know there is a funeral to be held this evening, at the Bukit Besar? Do you know whose funeral it is? The half-Dutch girl, Mina.'

'Mina! She's dead?' exclaimed Tyne.

'That is generally the reason for funerals,' said Amir caustically. 'The Rosks killed her because she had to do with your friend Mumford. Perhaps you will be interested to hear that the Rosks came for me yesterday; they tortured me. Perhaps today they will come back to kill me. You came to the Merdeka yesterday and I avoided you. Today I have not avoided you, and I shall probably die.'

'Nonsense, Amir, take a grip of yourself! The Rosks won't want you again,' Tyne said. 'What did they ask you yesterday?'

Amir stopped crying as suddenly as he had begun. Looking Tyne straight in the eye, he pulled his bandaged arm from its sling and began to unwrap it. In a minute he produced it, exposing it with a penetrating mixture of horror and pride.

'The Rosks asked me where Murray Mumford is hiding,' Amire said. 'Because I did not tell them, this is what they did to me.'

His left hand had been amputated at the wrist. Grafted on in its place, hanging limply, uselessly, was a chimpanzee's paw.

Tyne's own artificial left hand clenched convulsively in sympathetic pain.

'I'm sorry,' he said. 'I'm sorry, Amir.'

'This is how they think of man.'

He turned away, clumsily rebandaging his limb, and added in a choked voice, 'But I did not tell them where Murray is. You I can tell. When he came here early yesterday morning, he said he was going to hide in the old Deli Jalat temple, down the lane. Now please go. Go and do not ever ask me anything again.'

'I'm truly sorry,' Tyne said, pausing by the door. 'This'll be made up to you one day, Amir. Wait and see.'

Amir did not turn round.

*　　*　　*

Outside, Tyne leapt straight over a low stone wall and crouched there with his gun out. Amir had given him a bigger shaking than he cared to admit to himself. Slowly he raised his head and looked about.

One or two natives were busy about the few dwellings facing on to the little back street into which he had emerged; none of them seemed to be interested in Murray. With a pang, he realised a bitter truth in what Amir had said. To the local population, the visiting nations which had descended upon Sumatra were as troublesome as the Rosks. Both groups were equally opposed to their way of life. The Rosks owed their ability to travel easily beyond their perimeter to a typically Eastern indifference to which of two forms of explanation fell upon them. Had the powerful Western nations behaved with more consideration to Sumatra over the past few centuries, they might be receiving more consideration from her now.

As Tyne was about to climb back over the wall, a man appeared from the direction of the Merdeka. He walked slowly as befitted his bulk, his eyes guardedly casting to left and right. It was Stobart.

He was walking away from the direction in which the Deli Jalat temple stood. When he saw the road was empty, he quickened his pace. As Tyne sank back into concealment, Stobart produced a whistle, raised it to his lips, blew it. No audible sound emerged; it was ultrasonic – no doubt a summoning of forces.

Directly the U.N.C. agent had gone, Tyne hopped back over the low wall and headed in the direction of the temple, where Murray had told Amir he was going to hide. The settlement with Murray was coming; in Tyne's pocket, the loaded gun felt reassuringly heavy.

Despite the hot sun on his shoulders, icy clarity seized him. He knew exactly what he was going to do. He was going to kill Murray.

Only one thing worried him, and he wasn't going to let that spoil his aim. Murray, waiting with his microfilm to meet the RPF agent, had covered his tracks well; the glimpse of Stobart (who had no doubt picked up Tyne's trail in the Merdeka lounge) was a token he was still at large, despite the none too scrupulous powers ranged against him. Yet Tyne, working alone, was on the point of finding him. Why?

Two pieces of information had led Tyne to Murray: Mina's information about the 'plankton plant'; and from there, Amir's about the temple. Both U.N.C. and, presumably, Rosk had got the same lead from Mina; neither had got anything from Amir. Mina's information was capable of correct interpretation *only by Tyne;* Amir had said his piece voluntarily *only to Tyne.* Why?

One answer alone emerged. Murray had expected Tyne to pursue him. Before going into hiding, he had left those two

62

messages with Mina and Amir deliberately *knowing Tyne would follow them up.* Yet Murray would realise Tyne could have only one reason for following: to avenge Allan Cunliffe's death on the moon. And the motives a man might have for silently, deviously, beckoning his murderer towards him remained notably obscure. And seductively obscure.

Murray must be made to explain before the stolen gun and the bought bullets had their way with him. He must explain – and of course he must yield up the vital microfilm; then he could die. Tyne experienced that touch of ice-cold clarity again. Once more he was right in the torrid zone of events. The equator of action whirled faster and faster about him; yet he could not feel a thing.

*　　*　　*

'Come in, sir. I will make inquiry about your friend from the priests,' the wizened dwarf at the teak gate said. He pattered away on bare feet, crabbed and eager. Fallen women and white tuans especially welcome.

The Deli Jalat temple stood decaying in several acres of ground which were littered with past attempts to start chicken farms and scrap heaps. The central building was a not ignoble imitation of a late Hindu temple, highly ornamented, but round it had collected, like smashed cars round a road obstruction, a number of later erections, most of them flimsy affairs of lath or corrugated iron. These had never been immaculate; now they were merely tumbledown.

Unwilling to wait where he was bidden, Tyne moved over grass-encircled stones after the gatekeeper. In the air lingered an enchantingly sweet-sharp smell, a scent that seemed to carry with it its own unidentifiable emotion. There was a spice garden – grown out of hand, no doubt! close at hand. Turning a corner, Tyne came on a ramshackle covered way. At the far end, a woman in a Chinese dress, with clacking wooden soles on her feet, turned to look at him, then ran through a doorway. It looked like – yes, it had looked like Benda Ittai. Instinctively, Tyne increased his pace, sunlight jogging up and down on his shoulders.

He had a sudden choking image of taking her into the deserted spice garden, of making love to her there. It was not a picture he had intended. He turned his thoughts to Murray.

At the last door, the gatekeeper almost fell upon him with excitement, waving his arms anxiously.

'No sir, not here, sir! Stop by the gate, sir. Previously I ask you to wait. The priests will not be prepared –'

'I've not come to see the priests,' Tyne said. Pushing the man aside, he stepped in, into the shade inside the building. It was as if the sunlight had rattled up like a blind, showing the room behind it: a cool room, all wood, except for two big stone vases in the middle of the floor. Three men, priests, with that vindictive, forward-leaning air that religion implants in the elderly, came forward at once.

'Please take me to Murray Mumford. I cannot wait.' Tyne said.

'This is not a suitable hour,' one of them said, ineffectually waving his hands.

'I'm sorry I cannot wait.'

The three priests broke into a dialect, chattering rapidly to each other. They were frightened and angry. Fright won.

'Better to follow me,' one of them said, beckoning querulously at Tyne.

He led the way up broad and creaking stairs, on which a smell of cats floated. They passed down corridors of wood and corridors of stone, finally stopping by an insignificant door below another staircase. The priest unbarred this door and opened it. A short anteroom was revealed beyond, with two doors leading from it.

'Try the right door,' suggested the priest.

As Tyne stepped inside, the priest slammed the door behind him. Left suddenly in semi-darkness, he moved, carefully over to the right-hand door; steadying himself, levelling the gun, he flung the door open.

It was a long, narrow room with a dirty window at one end. Occupying most of the space near the door was a wooden bed, now in use as a table and seat combined.

Benda Ittai, in a Chinese dress, stood alone in the middle of the room, her mouth slightly open in a *moue* of surprise.

'Come in, Mr Todpuddle,' she said, using the name Tyne had assumed when interrogated on Budo Budda's ketch.

He nodded to her, as if in brief acknowledgement of her beauty.

His hackles up, Tyne took one step inside the room. Murray Mumford stood behind the door, his hands raised above his head. Round his waist he wore a Space Service belt; a revolver protruded from its unbuttoned holster.

Tyne swung slowly on his heel, bringing his own revolver up to cover Murray's chest. He was aware of his face, stiff as leather, contorted into a killer's grin.

'Glad you finally made it, Tyne,' Murray said, with a fair attempt at his old manner. 'Put your gun away and make yourself at home. Welcome to my humble –'

'Move over by the girl,' Tyne said in a rasping whisper. 'And I'll have your gun. Keep your hands raised. You're scum, Mumford – a betrayer, a traitor.'

'If you hadn't got that toy in your hand I'd break your neck for saying that,' Murray said evenly, his cheeks colouring darkly.

'No, you wouldn't! Are you suggesting you aren't carrying information for the Rosks – information absolutely vital to Earth?'

Murray, keeping his hands raised, looked at Tyne straightly as he shuffled over towards Benda. His roughly handsome face looked tired and shadowy.

'If you want to discuss it, throw both the guns up on that high shelf,' he said.

The shelf he referred to ran along one wall by the ceiling. Tyne never even glanced at it. He had the two of them together now, standing awkwardly by the foot of the bed.

'I don't want to discuss anything with you, Murray,' he said.

'Go ahead and shoot me, then. But you probably realise as well as I do that one fool move like that and everything is lost.'

'Give me that spool of microfilm, Murray.'

'I've not got it!'

Tyne jerked his revolver convulsively. That he had not expected.

'Stop!' Benda Ittai made a nervous move forward. Though haggard, she still looked impressively cool and beautiful. 'There is no time for quarrels, or we may be trapped here. Mr Leslie, put both of the guns on the shelf and then we can explain to you. It is really necessary.'

Tyne hesitated. He was in an awkward spot and he knew it. The vital matter was not his personal urge for revenge, but the need to get the film. The Rosk woman at least made it possible for him to back down without losing too much face. Roughly, he snatched Murray's revolver from its holster and threw it up on the shelf with his own.

'Better,' Murray said, lowering his hands and fumbling for mescahales. Tyne noted with satisfaction how those hands trembled as they lit the tube. His own hands – even his steel one – were trembling in the same way.

Taking the initiative again, he said to Benda, 'I assume from your presence here that you are the Rosk agent Murray was told to meet?'

She said: 'That is correct; as you know, I was held up.' She smiled slightly, with satisfaction at the understatement.

Murray said: 'You guess right; now stop guessing and listen to me. We may have very little time and we need your help.'

'My help!' Tyne exploded. 'I came here to kill you, Murray, by God, and now you tell me –'

Benda Ittai laid her hand on Tyne's arm. It felt soft and hot. 105.1, of course.

'Please give him a chance to explain!' she begged. 'Don't talk so much: listen! Just listen!'

'Yes, sound advice to an ex-politician!' Murray said. He was quickly getting control of himself. Tyne also savagely, wildly, took control of himself, sat on the edge of the plank bed and took a mescahale from Murray.

'Make it good,' he said. 'Make it very good.'

'The microfilm must be handed to Miss Ittai,' Murray said, 'and she must get it to Sumatra base, to the RPF there. Remember Tawdell Co Barr, the first Rosk to speak to Earth? He's the Peace Faction leader, secretly opposing Ap II Dowl. The RPF is weak; here is the one last chance to strengthen them to the point where they might overthrow Dowl. If they could show this microfilm, this proof of Dowl's bloody-mindedness, to a majority of the Rosks, the population would rise and rebel against the dictator.'

'Our people are as human as yours,' Benda broke in. 'Please see this terrible business as a moral struggle rather than a detective game. When their eyes are opened to what is going on behind their backs, all my people will surely rise against Dowl.'

'You're trying to tell me they don't know they're merely the advance party of an invasion?'

'Of course they don't. Can't you see,' she said desperately, 'we were all born on the ship, thinking ourselves colonists. There must have been sealed orders passed down from one generation of the officer class to the next.'

'I see,' Tyne said. He did see; this is how political manoeuvres must be carried out anywhere in the galaxy. The leaders plotted, and the rest followed like sheep – unless they could be roused to see that only muttonhood awaited them.

'You already have proof that I am no friend of Ap II Dowl and his ruffians,' Benda said, speaking quietly, probably conscious of the effect she had upon Tyne. 'Therefore trust me. Let me take the microfilm to my people, the RPF. There it will be used to more effect than if World Government got it. Can you see that?'

Yes, it was all clear enough, Tyne thought bitterly, knowing the other two were searching his face for a clue in advance to what he was going to say. He did not know what he was going to say. The issue – get the microfilm or bust! – had disintegrated as he approached it. Now he was faced with as ticklish a problem as ever he had met across the highly polished tables of the U.N.C.

If he did nothing – say, if he were shot – Under-Secretary Grierson would start the machinery grinding. The small Rosk force on Earth would be crushed before reinforcements arrived. And when they did arrive? Why, they would presumably be merciless: nuclear bombardment from space did not bear thinking of.

If Stobart and his men arrived here, they of course would take the microfilm without delay; they would find it wherever it was concealed. It would never go near a Rosk again. That move would also entail an immediate counter-attack against the perfidious alien within the gates.

If Ap II Dowl's men arrived here first – well, that was obviously the worst alternative of all.

At present, however, the initiative was not with Grierson, Stobart or Dowl; it was with Tyne. Fleetingly, he remembered the Theory of Irresponsible Activity he had formulated; he must have been light-headed at the time. Here he was faced with the weightiest problem of all time; how was he to resolve it for what would ultimately prove the best?

Turning towards the window, he gazed irritably out through the dusty panes, to hide his indecision from Murray and the girl. In the bright landscape outside, something moved. A man – or a Rosk – had dodged from one clump of bushes to another. Tyne's time was running low.

Abruptly, he turned back into the dull room. The RPF ought to have knowledge of the invasion plans, as Benda suggested; the more dissension sown in Sumatran Base, the better. Equally, Earth must have the details; then, they could be prepared for eventualities.

'A copy must be made of the microfilm, Miss Ittai,' he said. 'The U.N.C. will keep the copy to study. You will then be given safe conduct to slip back into your base with the original, to hand over to Tawdell Co Barr.'

67

He turned to Murray, sitting now on the edge of the bed, stubbling out his mescahale.

'As you observed, time is short,' he said. 'Give me the microfilm quickly.'

'You don't seem to take a point too well,' Murray said. He rubbed his eyes, looking tired and irritable: it was as if he had suddenly realised that whether he personally triumphed now or not, life would ultimately triumph over him – impersonally, of course, but with as little remorse as if the issue were a personal one! 'Lord Almighty, Tyne, isn't it obvious to you what a fool you are being? As I told you, I haven't got the microfilm.'

The bent figures running behind bushes – they would be straightening up now, perhaps making a last dash for the temple. And there was Allan Cunliffe, permanently straightened up, stiff as a stick. The two images, spears of urgency and anger, struck at Tyne's mind. He flung himself at Murray.

Murray got half up, then fell back under the assault. They crashed together on to the bed. The middle of it fell through, pitching them on to the floor. Tyne rolled on top of Murray. Doubled up, Murray ground his knee into Tyne's solar plexus. Tyne brought his steel hand chopping down on the side of Murray's neck. Blue about the lips, Murray subsided.

'That'll settle . . . your . . .' Tyne gasped. He had been badly winded. Blobs of colour waved like flags before his eyes. He shook his head to get the knocking sound out of it, before realising that someone was actually hammering on the door.

Looking up amid the ruins of the big bed, he saw Benda Ittai – but through a haze – open the door; one of the priests entered, speaking urgently to her. After a minute, she ran over to Tyne.

'The enemy are surrounding this building!' she said. 'The priests have seen them. Quickly, we must get away! I have a helicopter concealed outside. Come along!'

Seizing his good hand in her hot one, she pulled him to his feet. Murray groaned to himself as the weight shifted off him. Dazedly, Tyne allowed himself to be dragged from the room as the priest led them out. They trotted through the labyrinth of the building, Tyne gradually regaining his wits as they went. As they left the temple, he recalled that he had left his gun behind. It was too late to go back.

They emerged into a secluded courtyard surrounded by small cells once inhabited by novices. The whole place was slowly crumbling; it might have been built of old bread. Heat as choking as regret lay in the well of the mossy buildings. Under a stretched canopy of some camouflage material stood a small, trim helicopter. Benda ran across to it. She pressed one corner of the canopy and the whole thing collapsed, snapped up together like a blind. Picking it up, business-like, the girl stowed it into the helicopter and swung herself up.

She had an attractive pair of legs, Tyne thought. His powers of observation and deduction were returning. Even the sick feeling in his stomach was fading.

He pulled himself into the seat beside her as the priest backed bowing into the temple. At once, Benda started the rotors moving. They could see the disturbed heat move in whirlpools round them. Big green lizards scuttled for safety in the courtyard.

'Look!' Tyne shouted, pointing.

Over the top of a row of cells, a head appeared. Then shoulders. Then a rifle, swinging down to point into the helicopter. Rosk or man? Did Benda know? All she had said in the temple was, 'The enemy are surrounding us.' By that, she might have meant Ap II Dowl's toughs, or Stobart's. Which indicated the ambiguity of the role she played.

Almost jabbing her elbow into Tyne's ribs, Benda thrust her hand down into a capacious pocket. She had one of those murderous .88's there. Whipping it round, leaning half out of the cabin, she took a pot-shot at the sniper on the roof.

She missed.

Tyne saw the ridge of the roof shatter, spraying bits of tile into the sniper's face. His rifle went off wildly as he flung his hands up to his bleeding mouth. Then the helicopter began to rise.

As they began to bucket upwards, a man ran from the temple into the bright sunlight. It was Stobart, his face blistered with sweat, his great body heaving with exertion. Although he clasped a gun in one hand, he made no attempt to shoot; instead he was bellowing at Tyne, beckoning him savagely. Not a word came through the blanketing roar of the rotors above them.

'Just away in time!' Benda called.

Rising speedily about the ramshackle knot of temple buildings, they slanted eastwards and saw ant-sized men run into the open. Their shadow fled across the ants. The ants were firing upwards, fruitlessly.

VII

MOPPING his face, Tyne thought hard. It was obvious enough that the charming Miss Ittai, far from having saved his life again, as he had at first believed to be the case, had tricked him into getting into the helicopter. She had wanted, for reasons of her own, to get him away from his own people. His brain was still muzzy from the effect of Murray's knee in his stomach; savagely, he shook his head. Fuzzy he might be, but on several points he was clear enough. And one of them was: this little beauty was heading in the direction of the Roskian Sumatra Base as fast as she could go.

A little, round cloud formed ahead, and another beyond that. They hit turbulence and lumped heavily up and down. Someone below had an anti-flight gun trained on them.

Tyne looked down, but could see only roads and plantations. All round the outskirts of Padang, the U.N.C. Force had pockets of fortification and defence. Stobart must have worked, quickly in getting on to them. In a minute, Tyne thought, interceptors would be up after them. He did not relish the idea.

The same thought had occurred to the girl. Grimly, she was knocking every last spark of power out of the machine. Another crumpling explosion outside sent them rocking sideways. Locking the controls on a climbing course, she turned to Tyne. Suddenly, the gun was in her hand again.

'I hate to do this, but you must realise I will do anything to succeed, anything,' she said. 'This mission must be carried through at all costs. Beside it, none of us matter at all. If you so much as move suspiciously I will kill you. I will have to kill you.'

'You know, you interest me, Benda,' Tyne said. 'Why couldn't you have fallen in with the scheme for duplicating the microfilm I suggested back in the temple?'

She smiled dismissively. 'Do you really think your people would let you, me or the film go, once they had us? You are really an amateur, Tyne.'

'I've heard that said before, thanks. What do you want me to do?'

The craft bucked furiously as he asked. Hanging on, keeping the gun fixed on him, Benda said, 'It is getting rough. We are probably being pursued so you must bail out. There is one of our mini-rotor kits behind you, which is the equivalent of your parachutes. Put it on, jump! That will be a distraction to the U.N.C. Forces. Possibly when they see you are going down, they will cease to chase me. Also, this little flier will travel faster without you.'

'You have it all worked out,' Tyne said admiringly. 'And it can't be far to the Rosk base now. Anything else you want before I go?'

Her gun waved a little.

'Yes,' she said. 'Unscrew your false hand and give it to me.'

A wave of something like triumph ran over Tyne. So at last he had guessed, and guessed rightly. Benda had 'rescued' him for the same reason that Murray had deliberately left him a trail to follow: because Tyne was absolutely essential to their plan. All the time he had seemed to be on the fringe of events, he had been at the centre.

Murray had wanted a safe hiding place for the microfilm, somewhere where his contact could still get them even if he were intercepted. So when Tyne was unconscious on the trip back from Luna Area 101, it had been an easy matter for him to slip the little spool inside the cavity of one of Tyne's steel fingers. Then he had played on Tyne's feelings harshly enough to ensure the latter followed him, made himself conveniently accessible! All the time that Tyne had presumed himself to be acting under free will, to be daring all in the name of action, his moves had been calculated long in advance by someone else. The puppet had danced, unconscious of its strings.

Reading the anger and resentment on Tyne's face, Benda jerked the gun at him in warning.

'Fire!' he said. 'For God's sake, fire, girl! I'm less of an amateur than you think. When I thought about it, it was obvious why you left Murray behind at the temple instead of me; before

71

I broke in on the pair of you, he told you what he'd done about hiding the film, didn't he?'

'I'm sorry,' she said. 'You were rather sweet.' Shutting her eyes she fired at point blank range. He watched her little fist contract as she squeezed the trigger.

Tyne opened his good hand, showing her a palm full of the semi-self-propelled bullets.

'I emptied your gun while you were playing with the controls. I thought you might be dangerous; I was right, wasn't I?'

Unexpectedly, she burst into tears; they looked much like any girl's tears. Tyne did not realise at the time the relief those tears expressed; relief both at having done her duty and at having been baulked of the necessity for taking life. Pulling the gun from her hand, Tyne reloaded and thrust it into his own pocket.

Now he turned his attention to the helicopter.

The anti-flight barrage had dropped behind. They were over jungle now, still gaining height. Screwing his eyes against the sun's glare, Tyne peered back into the blue sky. Scudding behind them, a V-shape moved low over the variegated cover, gaining, climbing. It was a manned interceptor, coming after them fast.

It seemed to be a case of get down or be shot down. Tyne grabbed the controls, angling the rotors, letting them slide down the sky. He felt only exhilaration at that moment.

Away ahead, blue, hazy, an egg stuck out of the broken wash of landscape. It was the grounded Alpha II ship. They were that near Rosk Base! Tyne growled with a sort of pleasure. At least he had saved himself a visit there. Moreover, although at the eleventh hour, he had saved the situation; Benda sat helpless beside him, suddenly drained of will. He was in control now.

He felt more than heard the interceptor come up. Tyne jogged the wheel, letting them sideslip – but not out of danger. An air-charge burst above the cabin. The controls went dead instantly, their vital elements fused.

Tyne cursed as the helicopter jerked over on to its back, clouting his head against the brace. For a moment he became detached from the scene, watching as from a long distance while the Rosk girl wrenched helplessly at the panel. Then the jungle spun up, and he snapped back into full possession of his senses. They were about to crash!

'Hang on!' he yelled.

So he was in control, was he? – And this was what being in control consisted of: hanging on!

They struck!

In the terrifying concussion, shreds of pulpy green stuff flew everywhere. The helicopter split like matchwood. Yet they were lucky. They had crashed into a thicket of giant cactus, some pillars of which reared twenty-five feet high. The stuff acted like a great pulpy cushion, breaking their fall.

Groaning, Tyne rolled over. Benda sprawled on top of him. Dragging her with him, still groaning with mingled shock and relief, Tyne crawled out of the debris, pushed his way painfully through shattered cacti, and stood up. Groggily, he looked round him.

The helicopter had crashed on an old lava bed. Rutted and furrowed, it supported little in the way of vegetation except for the occasional thicket of cactus, which crept tenaciously along fault lines. It was as forbidding a landscape as could be imagined. A quarter of a mile away stood a low rampart: the fortified perimeter of Sumatra Base. Directly he saw it, Tyne dropped to his knees. It did not do to come within range of that place.

As he was trying to drag the unconscious girl behind a cactus cliff, a shadow swooped across him. The interceptor was coming in to land. It amazed him that there was still no activity from the Rosk base; they had been known to fire on any Earth plane flying so near the perimeter. Settling Benda down as comfortably as he could, Tyne ran back to meet his pursuer.

The interceptor had landed tail first on its buffers. Already the pilot was picking his way over the uneven ground towards Tyne: although his head was bent as he watched his footing over the lava, Tyne recognised him. Dodging behind some nearby columns of cactus, he drew Benda's gun and waited in ambush for him.

'Raise your hands!' he said, as the man appeared.

Startled, Allan Cunliffe did as he was told.

'You don't have to aim that thing at me, Tyne,' he said quietly. He bit his lips and looked round anxiously.

'I think I do,' Tyne replied. 'Until about ten minutes ago, I thought you were dead; now I want a few explanations from you.'

'Didn't Murray tell you I was still alive?'

'No, Murray didn't have time to tell me much. I worked this one out for myself, believe it or not. As soon as I knew Murray had tricked me into following him around, I guessed his tale about shooting you on Luna was a lie, the carrot that kept me going like a donkey; I had thought it unlikely to begin with. Obviously that means you're as implicated as he. Take your belt off.'

'My trousers will fall down.'

'Keep clear of the cactus then!'

'You're not pleased to see me, Tyne; you're all mixed up.'

'So mixed up I trust no one. I regard you as an enemy, Allan.'

Tyne took the belt and began to tie Allan's hands behind his back. As he worked, Allan talked, protesting.

'Listen, Tyne, you can trust me, just as you always could. Do you think I'd work for the Rosks in any way? I'll tell you this: I was a U.N.C. agent before I ever met you – even before I joined the Space Service. And I can prove I'm an agent. Look, the two men who caught up with you at the plankton plant, and were in the car when the fly-spy appeared –'

'Dickens and the dumb fellow?' Tyne asked. 'What about them?'

'I was the dumb one, Tyne! I had to keep masked and silent or you'd have recognised me.'

Allan stood there helpless now, his trousers sagging down to his knees. In sudden fury, Tyne pushed him over and knelt by him, grabbing his shirt in his fist.

'You bastard, Allan! *Why* couldn't you have spoken? Why've I had to go round in the dark all the time, nobody helping me?'

Allan tried to roll away from him, his face black.

'You still had to think I was dead then, in case you gave up the hunt for Murray,' he said. 'Time was short; we wanted you to keep driving ahead. Don't you see that when Dickens had given you a spot of necessary information, we were going to *let* you escape!'

'You could be lying now!'

'Why should I lie? You must have that microfilm now – you reached Murray; all that's needed is to get it to U.N.C. as quickly as possible. Hand it over to me and let's get back to safety.'

*   *   *

Tyne's heart jumped. So Allan – once his friend, now (caught in the no-man's land of intrigue) his rival – did not know how Murray had concealed the invasion plans. Grabbing him by his jacket front, Tyne dragged him until they were behind a cactus clump, out of sight of the Rosk base, still surprisingly silent and menacing.

'Tell me what happened on Area 101 when I was laid low,' he demanded. 'When you were supposed to have been killed.'

'It's no secret,' Allan said, 'You went out like a light when you were hit on the shoulder. Murray and I tried to carry you back to the ship and of course the Rosks caught us and disarmed us. There were only three of them – did you know that? – but in their far more efficient suits, they made rings round us. They told us that they and the fellow manning the searchlight were the only members of the peace faction, the RPF, supporting Tawdell Co Barr on Luna. But they'd managed to filch these plans; that was easy enough. The trouble was to get them to Earth – they were all three already under suspicion.

'When we heard the facts from them, Murray volunteered to take the spool to their Padang contact. To make sure he did so, they said they would hold me hostage. I watched Murray drag you back into the ship and leave.'

'How did you get away from them?' Tyne asked suspiciously.

'I didn't. They let me go of their own accord after a while. At first I thought it was for the reason they gave, that they could not keep me concealed anywhere from Ap II Dowl's secret police; but it wasn't. They wanted me loose so that I could set the World Government forces on to Murray. I made full pelt for U.N.C. HQ Luna in the stolen lunarider they gave me, and got through to Double K Four – the agent you know by the name of Stobart. By the time he picked you up in the bar of the Roxy, he had heard from me and knew roughly what was going on. Then I got back to Padang myself as quickly as possible, meeting up with Stobart and Dickens. By then –'

'Wait a minute,' Tyne said.

He could hear a whine growing louder in the sky. He had been listening for it. Other interceptors were heading this way. Allan looked up with hope in his eyes. Tyne had less than five minutes left.

'I don't know what you're talking about,' he said roughly to Allan. 'You tell me these Roskian pacifists let you go so that you could set our people on to Murray, just when everything depended on his getting through? How do you make sense of that?'

'The whole business was staged to look as if everything depended on Murray's getting through. In fact, those RPF boys were clever; they wanted Murray caught with the film on him. They never intended anything but that the plans should fall into Earth hands. If Murray had double-crossed them, so much better. Of course, Tawdell's agent here, the girl Ittai, didn't

75

know that; she went to meet Murray in all good faith.'

'Why go such a long way round about? Why didn't they just post the film, once they had stolen it, direct to U.N.C.?'

Allan laughed briefly.

'And who'd have believed it? You know how the political situation stands. If the film had been sent direct to us, it would probably have been dismissed as just another of Ap II Dowl's threats. The Area 101 RPF had even planted that strange object we had to investigate outside their dome as a bait; we happened to be the mice who came and sniffed at the cheese.'

Tyne stood up. He could see the interceptors now, three of them flying low. At any minute now, they would see the crashed helicopter and be coming down.

'You've made yourself clear,' he said to Allan. 'The whole episode has been a twist from start to finish, and I've had to take most of the twisting. Only one thing isn't clear to me.'

Hopefully Allan propped himself on one elbow and asked what that was.

'I don't know who I can trust but myself. Everyone else is playing a subtle double game.'

'You can trust Stobart, even if you refuse to trust me. He should be in one of those three interceptors.'

'I trust nobody, not even that fat slob Stobart!'

Stooping, he wrenched Allan's trousers off, tied them savagely round his ankles.

'Sweat it out, feller!' he advised. 'Your pals will be down in a couple of minutes to put your pants on. And don't forget to look after Benda Ittai. She's over by the crash. Meanwhile, I'm borrowing your machine.'

Ignoring Allan's shouts, he ran across the lava bed to the grounded interceptor. The other planes were wheeling overhead. As he pulled himself into the swing seat, the radio was calling.

'. . . Why don't you answer? What's happening down there?' It was Stobart's voice, harsh but recognisable.

Puffing, assuming Allan's voice as well as he could, Tyne flipped the speech switch and said, 'Regret delay . . . fight with Leslie. . . . I've got him tied up. . . . Come on down.'

'Have you got the microfilm? Murray Mumford reports that it's in Tyne's false hand.'

'I haven't got it. Come on down,' Tyne said, cutting the voice off. Switching on the feed, he tensed himself and eased in the jets. Rocking skywards, the interceptor responded perfectly; Tyne had flown these machines back in his training days.

With joy, he thought of the indecision that must be clouding Stobart's mind. Yes, Stobart would be suspicious. But Stobart would have to land to discover that was going on. Tyne found himself hoping that the guns of the Rosk base would open up. Just to give the agent a scare.

He checked the fuel, finding his tanks almost full. Excellent; he could get to Singapore, centre of World Government, in one hop. He was not going to unscrew his steel fist for anyone less than Governor-General Hjanderson of the U.N.C.

VIII

IT was, and the most scrupulous person must agree, a beautiful cell; commodious, with toilet and bathroom (complete with shower and massage unit) attached, it was furnished in impeccable if uninspired taste, and provided with books, visicube and pictures; there was air-conditioning, there was concealed lighting, but it was still a cell.

The food was excellent and Tyne had eaten well. The couch was comfortable and Tyne had slept well. The carpet was deep, and Tyne now walked restlessly back and forth upon it.

His left hand was missing.

He had been confined here for twenty hours. Arriving in Singapore shortly after two o'clock on the previous afternoon, he had been arrested at once, interrogated at length and shut in here. His questioners had been civil, removing his steel hand sympathetically, even apologetically. Since then, all his wants had been ministered to, his patience had been exhausted.

A knock came at the door. They knocked! It seemed the ultimate in irony. A slender man with a face the colour of an old pocket, dressed in a faultless suit, entered and attempted to smile at Tyne.

'Would you be so kind as to step this way to see Governor Purdoe?' he asked.

Tyne saved his wrath, carrying it almost gleefully behind the minion until he was ushered into a large, bare room where a uniformed octogenarian rose from behind a desk. This was Prison Governor Purdoe, a watchful man with a watchful smile arranged on his apple-clean face.

'How much longer am I going to be locked up here?' Tyne demanded, marching up to his desk. 'When am I going to see Hjanderson? What the devil do you want to talk to me about?'

'I am the governor of this institute', the old man said reprovingly, without removing his smile.

'Let's not bring class into this. All I want to know is am I or am I not a bloody hero? If I am, is this the sort of treatment you think I enjoy?'

'You are indeed a hero, Mr Leslie,' the governor said placatingly. 'Nobody denies it. Please sit down and smoke a mescahale and let some of the blood drain out of your head.'

Governor Purdoe came round from behind the desk. He stood in front of Tyne, looking at him until he seated himself; then he said, 'It may console you to know that your two associates in this affair, Murray Mumford and Allan Cunliffe, are also detained here. We are not sitting idly by. Your stories are being correlated.'

'All I'm saying is that there was no need to place me under lock and key to start with. I came here voluntarily, didn't I?'

The governor inclined his grey head.

'When you arrived, there was a general U.N.C. call out for you, dead or alive. You were fortunate, Mr Leslie, that we managed to get you and keep you safely before less enlightened parties reached you. An agent whom I believe you know as Stobart had reason to fear, when you tricked him yesterday, that you might have turned traitor. He merely took the precautions expected of him.'

'Don't mention Stobart to me, Governor! It brings me out in a rash. Just tell me what you wanted me for. Can I have my fist back?'

Governor Purdoe smiled a little bleakly. Seen close to, the smile was not attractive.

'Shortly,' he said: 'I summoned you here because I wanted in general to tell you that you are in the best place here – that far from being neglected, you are the prime mover in a lot of intense activity, most of which necessarily remains secret, even from you – and in particular to tell you that Governor-General Hjanderson will come to thank you personally as soon as possible. We believe you acted with excellent intentions, you see.'

Snorting, Tyne stubbed out his mescahale on the shiny desk top and jumped up. He topped Purdoe by a head, but the latter never moved.

'Governments!' he snapped. 'You people are all alike! Diplomacy and suspicion – nothing but! Nobody trusting anybody! Don't you take anything that happens at its face value?'

'You have run into a lot of trouble because you did just that,' the governor said. He turned away, walked round behind his desk, sat down with a hint of tiredness. His manicured right hand performed a gesture of contempt. 'There is no trust anywhere, Leslie. I regret it as much as you, but I face the fact. None of you young men are realists. These plans for the invasion from Alpha Centauri II – not a word about them must escape; that is just one good reason for your continuing to stay with us. Try – please try to think less of yourself, and reflect instead on the grave issues looming behind these plans. Sithers, conduct our guest back to his – room.'

The man with the dirty linen face came forward. Tyne shrugged his shoulders, making hopelessly towards the door; he knew he would get nothing out of Purdoe even if he squeezed him like a sponge. He had met the institutional type before.

In the doorway he paused.

'Just tell me one tiny, weeny little state secret, governor,' he begged. 'All that tale Allan Cunliffe told me about the Rosks really manoeuvring to get the microfilm in our hands – was that true or false?'

An odd expression – it might have been another smile – passed over the governor's face and vanished.

'Cunliffe has been an excellent agent for a number of years,' he said, 'and, though I grant you it does not necessarily follow, everything he told you was perfectly correct. The RPF wanted us to get the invasion plans. However, there was one minor point he missed, because he could not possibly have known it. The invasion plans themselves are probably false.'

*   *   *

The rest of the day passed with intolerable slowness for Tyne.

He reflected, as the governor had urged him to do, on the grave issues behind the Rosk invasion plans. One issue at least stuck out a mile. There had been no proof as yet that Alpha II's technology was far in advance of Earth's in this last decade of the twenty-second century: even the construction of a gigantic interstellar ship was, in theory at least, not beyond Earth's resources. But an interstellar invasion implied many things. It implied, surely, some form of faster-than-light communication between Ap II Dowl's force and Alpha II. It implied, too, a drive a good deal faster than the one professedly used to get the first ship here, for no invasion would be feasible between planets a two-generations' journey apart. It implied, undoubtedly, an integration of planetary resources vastly superior to anything Earth dreamed of, split as it was into numerous fractious nations. It implied, above all, an overweening confidence in success; as vast an undertaking as an interstellar invasion would never get under way unless the powers behind it considered it a fool-proof scheme.

The picture was not, Tyne admitted to himself, anything but gloomy. The role he had played in it shrank into the mere prologue to a whole volume of catastrophe.

But if the plans were false?

What did that mean? Had the RPF been tricked, perhaps, into believing that the belligerent forces would do one thing, whereas actually they intended to do another? Tyne, sitting hour after hour in his so comfortable, so commodious cell, could invent many such unhelpful questions to ask himself. Only the answers were beyond him.

If he disliked not knowing the answers, he disliked knowing the question even more.

On the third day of Tyne's imprisonment, he was summoned again to the governor's presence. He appeared in chastened mood before the old man.

'I've had no news,' he said. 'What's the general situation? Are the Rosks making a move?'

'The situation has changed very radically since we last met,' Purdoe said, his face crumpling into innumerable pleats as he smiled. 'And may I say, Mr Leslie, how glad I am that you no longer come into here clamouring for release. You have been thinking, I take it?'

Tyne sighed.

'I'm not really a man of action, governor, but that doesn't mean you have to be avuncular with me. What have you brought me here for this time?'

'Take a mescahale, young man. The Governor-General of the U.N.C., Mr Hjanderson, is here to see you; and I should advise you to watch your tongue for the occasion. Now please excuse me for a minute.'

He disappeared through a rear door with his sprightly old man's gait. To kill time, Tyne stared at the linen-faced attendant who had brought him here; the attendant fingered his tie and coughed.

Hjanderson, when he appeared, was instantly recognisable: dapper, fifty-ish, a little like a wolf with an expense account, smelling agreeably of the most fashionable shaving soap. He shook hands briskly with Tyne and sat down facing him, palms pressed on knees.

'I promised to come and see you,' he said, 'and I have kept that promise. I regret it has taken me so long to do. These have been days of crisis. Very grave crisis.'

'I'm pleased if I have been of any service. Perhaps I can have my hand back now, sir.'

Handersen brushed most of this aside.

'Service? Yes, Leslie, I think you played your part as you saw it. You were never more than partially in the picture, you know. We have received a great deal of help from the Roskian girl, Benda Ittai, whom you left for dead beside her crashed helicopter.'

With an effort, Tyne swallowed this blatant misrepresentation; his term with the U.N.C. had accustomed him to such gambits.

'Apart from the fact that I did not leave her for dead how is she? Where is she?' he asked.

'She is radiant; she is here,' Purdoe said, interrupting, coming up from behind his desk. With his thin, veined hand he touched – for whatever privately submerged reason of his own – the arm of the fur coat Benda wore, as he ushered her through the rear doorway and into the office.

'Benda!' Tyne exclaimed. Forgetting the Governor-General of the U.N.C., he went over to her and took her hands. Hot; 105.1; alien; but beautiful, and smiling in most tender fashion. He couldn't let her get away with it so easily.

'Haven't seen you since you tried to shoot me,' he said affably.

'The situation has changed,' she said, still smiling. The tormented look she had worn when putting him ashore on the island had entirely gone now.

'Since you appear to have lost interest in the political situation,' Hjanderson said dryly, rising to his feet, 'it remains for me only to tell you that you are now a free man, Mr Leslie. Moreover, I think I can mention that it is possible you may eventually get some sort of decoration; the E.D.C.E., probably.'

'I'll wear it all the time,' Tyne promised, 'but before you go, please tell me about the invasion – what's happening, what's been done about it?'

'Miss Ittai can tell you the details,' Hjanderson said smiling and extending a sharp hand. 'Now you must excuse me; I have a news conference to attend. I am, of course, delighted to have been able to see you. I wish you good luck for the future.'

'Of course,' Tyne murmured vaguely. He turned to Benda before Purdoe had shown the Governor-General out. 'I'd prefer to ask you this over a restaurant table, but what's been happening that I don't know about?'

'Perhaps the table can be arranged later,' she said. 'From now on – whether that is what I want or not – I am on your side of the fence. I cannot go back to my people. That is why I have told the Governor-General the truth as I have found it to be.

'The invasion plans, as I think you have heard, are false. And not they only. The RPF also was a spurious organisation! Don't mistake me – a lot of its members genuinely wished for peace between Rosk and Man as I did and still do myself. But Tawdell Co Barr is, and must always have been, a puppet of Ap II Dowl's. No doubt we should all have been wiped out when we had served our purpose.'

'Budo Budda was out to kill you as it was.' Tyne said.

'Oh quite; I was merely expendable, I fear. Even Budda would not have known the RPF was a dummy front – otherwise he would not have been after Murray. Only Ap II and Tawdell Co Barr are supposed to know.'

'And how did you find out?'

She shrugged her shoulders, her face puckered as she recalled that horrible moment of revelation.

'For some time, small events in the Base had made me suspicious, but I really knew what was happening when we crashed near Sumatra Base and they neither opened fire on us nor sent a party out to pick us up. Their silence could mean only one thing: the plans were intended only for U.N.C. eyes. They were false, designed only to scare Earth.'

'They certainly did that,' Tyne agreed. 'This clears up one point that has been bothering me. I'd been wondering what this spool of microfilm was doing on Luna in the first place. Obviously it was planted there where its journey to your base would attract maximum attention.'

Benda Ittai began to look moist about the eyes, as the treachery of her fellow beings struck her afresh. Turning to Purdoe, who stood sympathetically by, Tyne asked, 'What was Ap II Dowl's idea in all this?'

With a barely perceptible gesture, Purdoe led Tyne to the other side of the room.

'This is all very sad for the young woman,' he said in an official voice. 'You see the invasion scare was Dowl's last bluff. When confronted in the Council with our knowledge of the plans, he would probably have said that he would call the attacking fleet off if we'd give him all Sumatra, or perhaps Africa as well, or half the globe, or whatever his megalomaniac mind conceived. He's got nothing to back a real threat, Leslie. This was pure bluff from start to finish. You were really ill-advised, if I may say so, to get mixed up in it.'

'We've all been chasing around risking our necks,' Tyne said testily, 'just to serve Dowl's purpose. But how are you so *sure* it's all bluff?'

For answer, the governor pulled a message form from his pocket and unfolded it daintily. Tyne recognised the flimsy as a signal which had come through secret government channels.

'This arrived just before I summoned you,' Purdoe said. 'Please read it. You will find it enlightening.'

The message read: 'Circulation: Govt Levels A-C only and List 566 as specified. Text begins: Hoyle Observatory, Luna, confirms Alpha Centauri about to go nova. Increase to apparent magnitude Minus One expected by end of year. This temperature rise will be sufficient to render life on its planets untenable. Authoritative circles confirm that first signs of nova effect would have been observable locally three generations ago in sunspot and radio phenomena. Rosk ship may therefore be regarded as lifeboat; no doubt other lifeboats dispatched to other nearby systems. Therefore chances of invasion now highly improbable, repeat highly improbable. Suggested course of action: summit announcement of text of this action, with warning to Ap II Dowl to settle down or move on. Text ends. 10/10/2193 Luna-Singa-Beam Y.'

Tyne put the flimsy down, slowly, blankly. Round his head ran some lines from an historical solid, the name of which eluded him; 'Thus enterprises of great pith and moment, With this regard their currents turn awry. And lose the name of action.' Was it Shakespeare? He was confused; from the diplomatic point of view, this, of course, was a triumph. The Rosks stood revealed in all their weakness, and could now be squashed as Earth saw fit. Yet in Tyne's head, the picture of oceans steaming, babies cooking slowly in cellars, planets gradually turning to ashes, seemed to him something less than a happy ending.

'I must say I have marked you down.' Governor Purdoe said, regarding Tyne coldly, 'as rather a hard and impertinent young man. How typical of your generation that you should have no reaction of this great news!'

'Good heavens!' Tyne exclaimed. 'I was just thinking –'

'Forgive me if I interrupt; no doubt you were thinking of your own personal glory; I can read you like a book. When Governor-General Hjanderson gave you your freedom, I hoped it meant you would leave here at once. Will you please do so now? And one thing – please take Miss Ittai with you. I understand she has formed an attachment for you; for me, that will always remain the ultimate proof of Roskian misguidedness.'

Tyne looked hard at the old man, so neat, so smiling. With unexpected self-control, he swallowed his anger. He wanted to say that it would be impossible to understand a Rosk as long as it was impossible to understand a man, but the words did not come. There were no words; he realised he could comprehend Purdoe no more than Purdoe comprehended him.

Frustratedly, he turned to Benda Ittai. Here at least was someone worth trying to comprehend.

He felt like spending a life at it.

'Let's go and find that restaurant table I was telling you about,' he said, taking her arm.

She smiled at him. It was a very comprehensible smile.

SEGREGATION

by BRIAN ALDISS

AT other times of day, the pigmies brought the old man fish from the river, or the watercress which he loved, but in the afternoon they brought him two bowls of entrails. He stood to receive them, staring over their heads through the open door, looking at the blue jungle without seeing it. He was in pain. Yet he dared not let his subjects see that he suffered or was weak; the pigmies had a short way with weakness. Before they entered his room, he had forced himself to stand erect, using his heavy stick for support.

The two bearers stopped before him, bowing their heads until their snouts were almost in the still steaming bowls.

'Thank you. Your offering is received,' the old man said.

Whether or not they really comprehended his clicking attempt at reproducing their tongue, he could not tell. Shaking slightly, he patted their scaly heads, after which they rose and departed with their rapid, slithering walk. In the bowls, oily highlights glistened, reflected from the sunshine outside.

Sinking back on to his bed, the old man fell into his usual fantasy: the pigmies came to him, and he treated them not with forbearance but hatred. He poured over them the weight of his long-repressed loathing and despisal, striking them over the heads with his stick and finally driving them and all their race for ever from this planet. They were gone. The azure sun and the blue jungles were his alone; he could live where nobody would ever find or worry him. He could die at last as simply as a leaf falls from a tree.

The reverie faded, and he recognised it for what it was. He knotted his hands together till the knuckles stood out like cobble stones, coughing a little bood. The bowls of intestines would have to be disposed of.

Next day, the rocket ship landed a mile away.

*　　*　　*

The big overlander lumbered along the devious forest track. It was losing as little time as possible with Barney Brangwyn's expert hand at the wheel. On either side of the vehicle, the vegetation was thick, presenting that sombre blue-green hue which characterised most of the living things on the planet Kakakakaxo.

'You neither of you look in the pink of health!' Barney observed, flicking his eyes from the track to glance at the azure lights on the faces of his two companions.

The three members of the Planetary Ecological Survey Team (PEST for short) appeared to have blue snow-shadows shading every plane of their countenances; yet in this equatorial zone, and with the sun Cassivelaunus shining at zenith, it was comfortably warm, if not hot. The surrounding jungle grew thickly, with an almost tropical luxuriance, the bushes seeming to sag under the weight of their own foliage. It was strange to recall that they were heading for a man who had lived in these uninviting surroundings for almost twenty years. Now they were here, it became easier to see why he was universally regarded as a hero.

'There's plenty of cover here for any green pigmies who may be watching us,' Tim Anderson said, peering at the passing thickets. 'I was hoping to see one or two.'

Barney chuckled at the worried note in the younger man's voice.

'The pigmies are probably still getting over the racket we made in landing,' he said. 'We'll be seeing them soon enough. When you get as ancient as I am, Tim, you'll become less keen to meet the local bigwigs. The top dogs of any planet are generally the most obstreperous – ipso facto, as the lawyers say.'

He lapsed into silence as he negotiated a gulley, swinging the big vehicle expertly up the far slope.

'By the evidence, the most obstreperous factor on Kakakakaxo is the climate,' Tim said. 'Only six or seven hundred miles north and south of here, the glaciers begin, and go right on up to the poles. Admittedly our job is to vet the planet to see that it's safe for colonists to move in, but I shouldn't want to live here, pigmies or no pigmies; I've seen enough already to tell you that.'

'It's not a question of choice for the colonists,' Craig Hodges, leader of the team, remarked. 'They'll come because of some kind of pressure on them: economic factors, oppression, destitution, or the need for liebensraum – the sort of grim necessities which keep us all on the hop.'

'Cheer up, Craig!' Barney exclaimed. 'At least Daddy Dangerfield likes it here! He had faced Kakakakaxo for nineteen years, wet nursing his pigmies!'

'Don't forget he crashed here accidently in the first place; he's just had to adjust,' Craig said, unwilling to be shaken out of a melancholy which always descended on him when the PEST first confronted the mystery of a new planet.

'What a magnificent adjustment!' Tim exclaimed. 'Daddy Dangerfield, God of the Great Beyond! He was one of my childhood heroes. I'm greatly looking forward to seeing him.'

'Most of the legends built round him originated on Droxy,' Craig said, 'where half the ballyhoo in the universe comes from. I am chary about the blighter myself, but at least he should prove helpful to us – which is why we're going to look him up.'

'Of course he'll be helpful,' Barney said, skirting a thicket of rhododendron. 'He'll save us a wack of field work. In nineteen years – if he's anything like the man he's cracked up to be – he should have accumulated a mass of material of inestimable value to us. You can't tell me Daddy won't simplify our task enormously, Craig; don't be a pessimist.'

*   *   *

The PEST task was seldom simple. When a three-man team landed on an unexplored planet like Kakakakaxo, they had to categorise its possible dangers and determine exactly the nature of the opposition any superior species might offer to colonising man. The superior species, in a galaxy tumbling with diversity, might be mammal, reptile, insect, vegetable, mineral, or virus – but frequently it was, as Barney hinted, so obstreperous that it had to be obliterated entirely before man could move in – and exterminated so that the ecological balance of the planet was disturbed as little as possible.

Their journey ended unexpectedly. They were only a mile from their ship when the jungle on one side of the overlander gave way to a cliff, which formed the base of a steep and afforested mountain. Rounding a high spur of rock, they saw the pigmies' village ahead of them. When Barney braked and cut out the atomic motor, the three of them sat for a minute in silence, taking in the scene.

Rapid movement under the trees followed their arrival.

'Here comes the welcoming committee,' Craig said. 'We'd better climb down and look agreeable, as far as that is possible; Heaven knows what they are going to make of your beard, Barney. Get your gun on, Tim, just in case it's needed.'

Jumping to the ground, the trio were almost immediately surrounded. The pigmies moved like jerky lightning, enclosing the ecologists. Though they appeared from all quarters, apparently without prearranged plan, it took them only a few seconds to form a wall round the intruders. And for all their speed, there was a quality of stealth about them, possibly because they made no sound. Perhaps, Tim thought encouragingly to himself, it was because they were shy. Yet there was something menacing about their haste; they were ugly creatures.

They moved like lizards, and their skin was like lizard skin, green and mottled, except where it broke into coarse scales down their backs. Pigmy-sized, none of them stood more than four feet high. They were four-legged and two-armed. Their heads, perched above their bodies with no visible neck, were like cayman heads, fitted with long, cruel jaws and serrated teeth. These heads now swivelled from side to side, like gun turrets on tanks seeking sight of the enemy. It looked an apprehensive gesture.

Once they had surrounded the ecologists, the pigmies made no further move, as if the initiative had passed from them. In their baggy throats, heavy pulses beat.

Craig pointed at a cayman-head in front of him and said, 'Greetings! Where is Daddy Dangerfield? We intend you no harm. We merely wish to see Dangerfield. Please take us to him.'

He repeated his words in Galingua.

The pigmies stirred, opening their jaws and croaking. An excited clack-clack-clackering broke out on all sides. Overpoweringly, an odour of fish rose from the creatures. None of them volunteered anything which might be construed as a reply. The wave of excitement, if it was that, which passed over them emphasised their more formidable features. Their stocky bodies might have been ludicrous, but their two pairs of sturdy legs and, above all, their armoured jaws would deter anyone from regarding them as figures of fun.

'These are only animals!' Tim exclaimed. 'Look at them – they relieve themselves as they stand, like cattle. They possess none of the personal pride you'd expect in a primitive savage. They wear absolutely nothing in the way of clothes. Why they aren't even armed!'

'Don't say that until you've had a good look at their claws and teeth,' Barney said cheerfully. He had caught the loathing in the youngster's voice, and knew how often loathing cloaks fear. He himself felt a curious, dry tension, originating less from thought of the pigmies than from the reflection that the three of them were in an unknown world, without precedents to guide them; when he ceased to feel that tension, he would be due for retirement.

'Move forward slowly with me,' Craig said. 'We are doing no good just standing here. Dangerfield must be about somewhere, heaven help him.'

Thigh-deep in clacking caymen-heads, who kept them encircled, the PEST men advanced towards the settlement, which lay in patchy tones of blue sunshine and blue shade ahead. As far as they could tell, this manoeuvre was resented by the pigmies, whose noise redoubled. When they spoke, their grey tongues wagged up and down in their long mouths. They backed away without offering opposition. Following Craig's lead, Barney and Tim kept their hands above their sidearms, in case of trouble.

*   *   *

So they moved slowly into the village. The strange aspect of the place now became apparent. Bounded on one side by the cliff face, the village stood under trees which grew straight out of the dark soil. Up in the thick blueish foliage of these trees, an immense colony of gay-coloured birds, evidently a sort of weaver, had plaited a continuous roof out of lianas, climbers, leaves and twigs. Under this cover, on the dropping-bespattered ground, the pigmies had their rude huts, which were no more than squares of woven reed propped at any angle by sticks, to allow an entrance. They looked like collapsed bivouacs.

Tethered outside these dismal dwellings were furry animals, walking in the small circles allowed by their leashes and calling dolefully to each other. Their mewing cries, the staccato calls of the birds, and the croaking of the caymen-heads, made a babel of sound. And over everything lay the ripe stench of decaying fish.

'Plenty of local colour,' Barney remarked.

In contrast to this squalid scene was the cliff face, which had been ornately carved with stylised representations of foliage mingled with intricate geometrical forms. Later, the ecologists were to find that this work was crude in detail, but from a distance its superiority to the village was most marked. As they came nearer, they saw that the decorated area was actually a building hewn in the living rock, complete with doors, passages, rooms and windows, from the last of which pigmies watched their progress with unblinking curiosity.

'Impressive! Their claws can be turned to something else than attack.' Tim observed, eyeing the patterns in the rock.

'Dangerfield,' Craig called, when another attempt to communicate with the pigmics had failed. Only the whooping birds answered him.

Already the pigmies were losing interest. They pressed less closely round the men. Several scuttled with lizard speed back into their shelters. Looking over the knobby heads of the crowd, Barney pointed to the far side of the clearing. There, leaning against the dun-coloured rock of the cliff, was a sizeable hut, built of the same flimsy material as the pigmy dwellings, but evidently containing more than one room. As they regarded it, a man appeared in the doorway. He made his way towards them, aiding himself along with a stout stick.

'That's Dangerfield!' Barney exclaimed.

A warning stream of excitement ran through Tim. Daddy Dangerfield was something of a legend in this region of the inhabited galaxy. Crash-landing on Kakakakaxo nineteen years ago, he had been the first man to visit this uninviting little world. Kakakakaxo was off the trade routes, although it was only fifteen light years from Droxy, one of the great interstellar centres of commerce and pleasure. So Dangerfield had lived alone with the pigmies for ten standard years before someone had chanced to arrive with an offer of rescue. Then the stubborn man refused to leave, saying the native tribes had need of him. He had re-mained where he was, a God of the Great Beyond, Daddy to the Little Folk – as the sentimental Droxy tabloids phrased it, with their usual affection for titles and capital letters.

As he approached the team now, the pigmies fell back before

him, still maintaining their clacking chorus. Many of them slid away, bored by affairs beyond their comprehension.

*   *   *

It was difficult to recognise, in the bent figure peering anxiously at them, the young, bronzed giant by which Dangerfield was represented on Droxy. The thin, sardonic face with its powerful hook of nose had become a caricature of itself. The grey hair was long and dirty. The lumpy hands which grasped the stick were bespattered with liver marks. This was Dangerfield, but appearances suggested that the legend would outlive the man.

'You're from Droxy?' he asked eagerly, speaking in Galingua. 'You've come to make another film about me? I'm very pleased to see you here. Welcome to the untamed planet of Kakakakaxo.'

Craig Hodges put out his hand.

'We're not from Droxy,' he said. 'We're based on Earth, although most of our days are spent far from it. Nor have we come to make films; our mission is rather more practical than that.'

As Craig introduced himself and his team, Dangerfield's manner became noticeably less cordial. He muttered angrily to himself about Droxy.

'Come along over and have a drink with us in our wagon.' Barney said. 'We've got a nice little Aldebaran wine you might like to sample. You must be glad to see someone to talk to.'

'This is my place,' the old man said, making a move in the direction of the overlander. 'I don't know what you people are doing here. I'm the man who beat Kakakakaxo. The God of the Crocodile Folk, that's what they call me. If you had pushed your way in here twenty years ago as you did just now, the pigmies would have torn you to bits. I tamed 'em! No living man has ever done what I've done. They've made films about my life on Droxy – that's how important I am. Didn't you know that?'

Tim Anderson winced in embarrassment. He wanted to tell this gaunt relic that Dangerfield, the Far-Flung Father, the Cosmic Schweitzer, had been one of his boyhood heroes, a giant through whom he had first felt the ineluctable lure of space travel; he wanted to tell him that it hurt to have his legend destroyed. Here was the giant himself – bragging of his past, and bragging moreover, in a supplicatory whine.

They came up to the overlander. Dangerfield stared at the neat shield on the side, under which the words Planetary Ecological

Survey were inscribed in grey. After a moment, he turned pugnaciously to Craig.

'Who are you people? What do you want here?' he asked.

'We're a fact-finding team, Mr Dangerfield,' Craig said levelly. 'Our business is to gather data on this planet. Next to nothing is known about ecological or living conditions here. We are naturally keen to secure your help; you should be a treasury of information –'

'I can't answer any questions! I never answer questions. You'll have to find out anything you want to know for yourselves. I'm a sick man – I'm in pain. It's all I can do to walk, I need a doctor, drugs. . . . Are you a doctor?'

'I can administer an analgesic,' Craig said. 'And if you will let me examine you, I will try to find out what you are suffering from.'

Dangerfield waved a hand angrily in the air.

'I don't need telling what's wrong with me,' he snapped. 'I know every disease that's going on this cursed planet. I've got fiffins, and all I'm asking you for is something to relieve the pain. If you haven't come to be helpful, you'd best get out altogether!'

'Just what is or are fiffins?' Barney asked.

'None of your business. They're not infectious, if that's what's worrying you. If you have only come to ask questions, clear out. The pigmies will look after me, just as I've always looked after them.'

As he turned round to retreat, Dangerfield staggered and would have fallen, had not Tim moved fast enough to catch his arm. The old fellow shook off the supporting hand with weak anger and hurried back across the clearing. Tim fell in beside him.

'We can help you,' he said pleadingly. 'Please be reasonable.'

'I never had help, and I don't need it now. And what's more, I've made it a rule never to be reasonable.'

Full of conflicting emotion, Tim turned and caught sight of Craig's impassive face.

'We should help him.' he said.

'He doesn't want help,' Craig replied, not moving.

'But he's in pain!'

'No doubt, and the pain clouds his judgement. But he is still his own self, with his own ways. We have no right to take him over against his expressed wishes.'

'He may be dying,' Tim said. He looked defiantly at Craig. Then he swung away, and walked rapidly off, pushing past the few caymen-heads who still remained on the scene. Dangerfield, on the other side of the clearing, disappeared into his hut. Barney made to follow Tim, but Craig stopped him.

'Leave him,' he said quietly.

Barney looked straight at his friend.

'Don't force the boy,' he said. 'He hasn't got your outlook to life. Just go easy on him, Craig.'

'We all have to learn,' Craig observed, almost sadly. Then, changing his tone, he said, 'For some reason we have yet to discover, Dangerfield is unco-operative. From first impressions, he is unbalanced, which means he may soon swing the other way and offer us help; that we should wait for: I am interested to get a straight record of his nineteen years here.'

'He's stubborn,' Barney said, shaking his head.

'Which is the sign of a weak man. That's why Tim was unwise to coax him; it would merely make him more obdurate. If we ignore him, he will come to us. Until then, we work on our own here, studying the local life. Firstly, we must establish the intelligence status of the pigmies, with a view to finding out how much opposition they will offer colonists. One or two other odd features may also prove interesting.'

*　　*　　*

Thrusting his hands in his pocket, Barney surveyed the tawdry settlement. Now that it was quieter, he could hear a river flowing nearby. All the pigmies had dispersed; some lay motionless in their crude shelters, only their snouts showing the blue light lying like a mist along their scales.

'Speaking off the cuff, I'd say the pigmies are subhuman,' Barney remarked, picking from his beard an insect which had tumbled out of the thatched trees above them. 'I'd also hazard they have got as far, evolutionwise, as they're ever going to get. They have restricted cranial development, no opposed thumb, and no form of clothing – which means the lack of any sexual inhibition, such as one would expect to find in this Y-type culture. I should rate them as Y gamma stasis, Craig, at first blush.'

Craig nodded, smiling, as if with a secret pleasure.

'Which means you feel as I do about the cliff temple,' he said, indicating with his grey eyes the wealth of carving visible through the trees.

'You mean – the pigmies couldn't have built it?' Barney said. Craig nodded his large head.

'The caymen-heads are far below the culture level implied by this architecture. They are its caretakers, not its creators. Which means, of course, that there is – or was – another species, a superior species, on Kakakakaxo, which may prove more elusive than the pigmies.'

Craig was solid and stolid. He had spoken unemphatically. But Barney, who knew something of what went on inside that megacephalous skull, realised that by this very way Craig had of tossing away an important point, he was revealing a problem which excited his intellectual curiosity.

Understanding enough not to probe on the subject, Barney filed it away for later and switched to another topic. For such a bulky specimen of manhood, he possessed surprising delicacy; but the confines of a small spaceship made a good schoolroom for the sensibilities.

'I'm just going to look at these furry pets the cayman-heads keep tied up outside their shelters,' he said. 'They're intriguing little creatures.'

'Go carefully,' Craig cautioned. 'I have a suspicion the cayman-heads may not appreciate your interference. Those pets may not be pets at all; the pigmies don't look like a race of animal-lovers.'

'Well, if they aren't pets, they certainly aren't cattle,' Barney said, walking slowly among the crude shelters. He was careful to avoid any protruding pigmy protruding snouts, which lay along the ground like fallen branches. Outside most of the shelters, two different animals were tethered, generally by their hind legs. One animal, a grey, furry creature with a pushed-in face like a pekinese dog, stood almost as high as the pigmies; the other animal, a pudgy-snouted little creature with brown fur and a gay yellow crest, was half the size of the 'peke', and resembled a miniature bear. Both pekes and bears had little black monkey-like paws, many of which were now raised as if in supplication as the ecologists approached.

'Certainly they are more attractive than their owners,' Craig said. Stooping, he extended a hand cautiously to one of the little bears. It leapt forward and clutched the hand, chattering in appealing fashion.

'Do you suppose the two species, the pekes and the bears, fight together?' Barney asked. 'You notice they are kept tied just far enough apart so that they can't touch each other. We may have found the local variation on cockfighting.'

'Bloodsports might be in accord with the looks of the pigmies,' Craig said, 'but not with the character of these creatures. Even their incisors are blunt. They have no natural weapons.'

'Talking of teeth, they exist on the same diet as their masters,' Barney commented.

The little animals were sitting disconsolately on decaying piles of fish bones, fish heads and scales, amid which irridescent beetles scuttled, busy almost beneath Barney's feet.

'I'm going to try taking one of these pekes back to the over-lander,' he announced. 'It should be well worth examining.'

*　　*　　*

From the corner of his eye, he could see a pigmy snout sticking out of its shelter not three yards away; keeping it under observation, he bent down to loosen the tightly-drawn thong from the peg in the ground. The tethered creatures nearby, large and small, set up an excited chatter as they perceived what Barney was attempting. At the same time, the watching pigmy moved.

Its speed was astonishing. One second it was scarcely visible in its shelter, its nose extended along the ground; the next, it confronted Barney with its claws resting over his hand, its ferocious teeth bared in his face. Small though the reptile was, undoubtedly it could have snapped his neck through. Its yellow eyes glared unblinkingly up at Barney.

'Don't fire or you'll have the lot on us,' Craig said, for Barney's free hand had gone immediately for his gun.

Almost at once, they found themselves surrounded by pigmies, all scuttling up and clacking excitedly. They made their typical noises by waggling their tongues without moving their jaws. Though they crowded in, apparently hostile, they made no attempt to attack Craig and Barney. Then one of them thrust forward and waving his small upper arm, commenced to harangue them.

'Some traces of a primitive speech pattern,' Craig observed coolly. 'Let me try a little barter for your pet, Barney, while we have their attention.'

Dipping into one of the pouches of his duty equipment, he produced a necklace in whose marble-sized stones spirals of colour danced, delicate internal springs ensuring that their hues changed continually as long as their wearer moved. It was the sort of bauble to be picked up for a few minicredits on almost any civilised planet. Craig held it out to the pigmy who had delivered the speech.

The pigmy leader scrutinised it briefly, then resumed his

harangue. The necklace meant nothing to him. With signs, Craig explained the function of the necklace, and indicated that he would exchange it for one of the little bears; but abundant though these animals were, their owners showed no sign of intending to part with one. Pocketing the necklace, Craig produced a mirror.

Mirrors unfailingly excite the interest of primitive tribes – yet the pigmies remained unmoved. Many of them began to disappear, speeding off with the nervous, lizard movements. Putting the mirror away, Craig brought out a whistle.

It was an elaborate toy, shaped like a silver fish with an open mouth. The pigmy leader snatched it from Craig's hand, leaving the red track of its claws across his open palm. It popped the whistle into its mouth.

'Here, that's not edible!' Craig said, instinctively stepping forward with his hand out. Without warning, the pigmy struck. Perhaps it misinterpreted Craig's gesture and acted, as it thought, in self-defence. Snapping its jaws, it lunged out at Craig's leg. The ecologist fell instantly. Hardly had he struck the ground when a blue shaft flashed from Barney's blast-gun. As the noise of the thermonuclear explosion rattled round the clearing, the pigmy topped over and fell flat, smoking.

In to the ensuing silence broke the terrified clatter of a thousand weaver birds, winging from their homes and circling high above the tree tops. Barney bent down, seized Craig round the shoulders, and raised him with one powerful arm, keeping the blaster levelled in his free hand. Over Craig's thigh, soaking through his torn trousers, grew a ragged patch of blood.

'Thanks, Barney,' he said. 'Let's get back to the overlander.'

They retreated, Craig limping painfully. The pigmies made no attempt to attack. They mostly stood still, crouching over the smoking body and either staring fixedly or waving their snouts helplessly from side to side. It was impossible to determine whether they were frightened by the show of force or had decided that the brief quarrel was no affair of theirs. At last they bent over their dead comrade, seized him by his hind feet, and dragged him briskly off in the direction of the river.

When Barney got Craig on to his bunk, he stripped his trousers off, cleansed the wound, and dressed it with antiseptic and restorative powder. Although Craig had lost blood, little serious damage had been done; his leg would be entirely healed by morning.

'You got off lightly,' Barney said, straightening up. 'It's a deep flesh wound, but that baby could have chewed your knees off if he had been trying.'

Craig sat up and accepted a mescahale.

'One thing about the incident particularly interested me,' he said. 'The cayman-heads wanted the whistle because they mistook it for food; fish obviously is the main item of their diet. The mirror and necklace meant nothing to them; I have never met a backward tribe so lacking in simple, elementary vanity. Does it connect with the absence of any sexual inhibitions which you mentioned?'

'What have they to be vain about?' Barney asked. 'After five minutes out there, I feel as if the stench of fish has been painted on me with a brush.'

Five minutes later, they realised Tim Anderson was nowhere in the overlander. Craig pursed his lips.

'Go and see if you can find him, Barney,' he said. 'I don't like to think of him wandering about on his own.'

The afternoon was stretching the blue shadows across the ground. In the quiet, you could almost hear the planet turn on its cold, hard axis. Barney set out towards the distant murmur of water, his face anxious. He turned down a narrow track among the trees, then stopped, unsure of himself. He called Tim's name.

An answer came almost at once, unexpectedly. In a minute, Tim emerged from the bushes ahead and waved cheerfully to Barney.

'You had me worried,' Barney confessed. 'It's wiser not to stroll off like that without telling us where you are going to. What have you been doing?'

'Only taking a preliminary look round,' Tim said. 'The river's just beyond these bushes, wide and deep and fast-flowing. Do you think these cayman-heads could be cold-blooded by any chance?'

'They are,' Barney confirmed. 'One of them put a paw on my hand, and I observed a complete lack of heat in it.'

'Just as well for them,' Tim remarked. 'That river water is ice cold. It must flow straight down off the glaciers. The pigmies are superb swimmers, very fast, very sure; they look altogether more graceful in the water than they do on land. I watched them diving and coming up with fish the size of big salmon in their mouths.'

Barney told him about the incident with the fish-whistle.

'I'm sorry about Craig's leg,' Tim said. 'Perhaps you can tell me why he's got his knife into me, and why he jumped at me when I went after Dangerfield?'

'He hasn't got his knife into you. When you've been on this team a little longer, Tim, you'll see that Craig Hodges doesn't work like that at all. He's a neutral man. At present he's worried because he smells a mystery, but is undecided where to turn for a key to it. He probably regards Dangerfield as that key; certainly he respects the knowledge the man must have, yet I think that inwardly he would prefer to tackle the whole problem with a clean slate, leaving Dangerfield out of it altogether.'

'Why should Craig feel like that? PEST H.Q. instructed us to contact Dangerfield.'

'Quite. But Craig probably thinks the old boy might be – well, misleading, ill-informed . . .'.

They turned and began to make their way back to the settlement, walking slowly, enjoying the mild air uncontaminated by fish.

'Surely that wasn't why Craig was so ragged about helping Daddy Dangerfield?' Tim asked.

Barney sighed and tugged at his beard.

'No, that was something else,' he said. 'You develop a certain outlook to things when you've been on the PEST run for some years because a way of life induces an attitude to life. PEST teams are the precursors of change, remember. Before we come, the planets are in their natural state – that is, unspoiled or undeveloped, whichever way you phrase it. After us, they are going to be taken over and altered, on our recommendation. However cheery you feel about man's position in the galaxy, you can't help a part of you regretting that this inevitable mutilation is necessary.'

'It's not our business to care,' Tim said, impatiently.

'But Craig cares, Tim. The more planets we survey, the more he feels that some mysterious – divine – balance is being overthrown. I feel it myself; you'll grow to feel it in time; directly you land on an unmanned planet, an occult sense of *secrecy* comes up and hits you. . . . You can't avoid the idea that you are confronting an individual entity – and your sworn duty is to destroy it, and the enigma behind it, and turn out yet another assembly-line world for assembly-line man.

'That's how Craig feels about planets and people. For him, a man's character is sacrosanct; anything that has *accumulated* has his respect. It may be simpler to work with people who are mere ciphers, but an individual is of greater ultimate value.'

'So that's what he meant when he said Dangerfield was still his own self, I suppose.'

'More or less,' Barney agreed.

'Hm. All this business about attitudes to life seems a bit mystical to me.'

'Not a bit of it!' Barney said emphatically. 'It's damn practical. You take it from me, that when we've eventually taken Kaka-kakaxo to bits to see what makes it tick, we shall have nothing but a lot of integrated attitudes to life on our hands!'

'And a stink of fish,' Tim said sceptically.

'Even a stink of fish has –' Barney began, and broke off. The silence was torn right down the middle by piercing screams. The two ecologists looked at each other and then ran down the trail, bursting full tilt into the clearing.

Under the spreading thatch of the treetops, a peke creature was being killed. An excited rabble of pigmies milled everywhere, converging on a large, decaying tree stump, upon which two of their kind stood in full view, the screaming peke held tightly between them.

The furry prisoner struggled and squealed, while to its cries were added those of all the others tethered nearby. The screaming stopped abruptly. Without fuss, cruel talons came up and ripped its stomach open. Its entrails were scooped steaming, into a crudely shaped bowl, after which the ravaged body was tossed to the crowd. With delighted cries, the pigmies scrambled for it.

Before the hubbub had died down, another captive was handed up to the executioners, kicking and crying as it went. The crowd paused briefly to watch the fun. This time, the victim was one of the little bear-like animals. Its body was gouged open, its insides turned into a second bowl. It, too, was tossed to the cayman-headed throng.

'Horrible!' Tim exclaimed. 'Horrible!'

'Good old Mother Nature!' Barney said angrily. 'How many more of the little blighters do they intend to slaughter?'

But the killing was over. The two executioner pigmies, bearing the bowls of entrails clumsily in their paws, climbed from the tree stump and made their way through the crowd, which ceased its squabbling to fall back for them. The vessels were carried towards the rear of the village.

'It almost looks like some sort of a religious ceremony,' Craig said. Barney and Tim turned to find him standing close behind them. The screaming had lured him from his bed; in the tumult, he had limped over to them unobserved.

'How's the leg?' Tim asked.

'It'll be better by morning, thanks. I can feel it beginning to heal already.'

'The fellow who bit you – the one Barney killed – was thrown into the river,' Tim said. 'I was there watching from the bank when the others turned up with his carcass and slung him in.'

'They're taking those bowls of guts into Dangerfield's hut,' Barney said, pointing across the clearing. The two cayman-headed bearers had disappeared; a minute later they emerged, empty-handed, from the hut by the cliff, and mingled with the throng.

'I wonder what the old boy wants guts for,' Tim said.

'Good God! The hut's on fire!' Craig exclaimed. 'Tim, quick and fetch a foam extinguisher from the vehicle. Run!'

A ball of smoke, followed by a licking flame, had shown through Dangerfield's window. It died, then sprang up again. Craig and Barney ran forward as Tim dashed back to the over-lander. The pigmies, some of whom were still quarrelling over the pelts of the dead peke and bear, took no notice of them or the fire as the men pelted past.

*　　*　　*

Arriving at the hut first, Barney burst in. The interior of the first room was full of smoke. Flame crawled among the dry rushes on the floor. A crude oil lamp had been upset; lying among the flames, it was clearly the cause of the outbreak. Only a few feet away, flat on his bed, lay Dangerfield, his eyes closed.

'He's fainted – and knocked over the lamp in doing so,' Craig said. Pulling a rug from the other side of the room, he flung it on to the fire and stamped on it. When Tim arrived with the extinguisher, a minute later, it was hardly needed, but they soused the smouldering ashes with it to make doubly sure.

'This might be an opportunity to talk to the old boy,' Craig said. 'Leave me here with him, will you, and I'll see what I can do.'

As Tim and Barney obeyed, Craig saw the two bowls of entrails standing on a side table. They were still gently steaming.

On the bed, Dangerfield stirred. His eyelids flickered.

'No mercy from me,' he muttered, 'you'll get no mercy from me.'

As Craig bent over him, his eyes opened. He lay looking up at the ecologist. Blue shadows lay like faded inkstains over the planes of his face.

'I must have passed out,' he said tonelessly . . . 'Felt so weak.'

'You knocked over your oil lamp as you went,' Craig said. 'I was just in time to save rather a nasty blaze.'

The old man made no comment, unless the closing of his eyes was to be interpreted as an indifference to death.

'Every afternoon they bring me the bowls of entrails,' he muttered. 'It's a . . . rite – they're touchy about it. I wouldn't like to disappoint them. . . . But this afternoon it was such an effort to stand. It quite exhausted me.'

Craig fetched him a mug of water. Dangerfield accepted, drinking without raising his head, allowing half the liquid to trickle across his withered cheeks. After a minute, he groaned and sat up, propping himself against the wall. Without comment, Craig produced a hypodermic from his emergency pack and filled it from a plastic phial.

'You're in pain,' he said. 'This will stop the pain but leave your head clear. It won't hurt you; let's have a look at your arm, can I?'

Dangerfield's eyes rested on the syringe as if fascinated. He began to shake slowly, until the rickety bed creaked.

'I don't need your help, mister,' he said, his face crinkling.

'We need yours,' replied Craig indifferently, swabbing the thin palsied arm. He nodded his head towards the bowls behind him. 'What are these unappetising offerings? Some sort of religious tribute?'

Unexpectedly the old man began to laugh, his eyes filling with tears.

'Perhaps it's to placate me,' he said. 'Every day for years, for longer than I can remember, they've been bringing me these guts. You wouldn't believe me if I told you, Hodges, that one of the chief problems of my life is hiding guts, getting rid of guts. . . . You see, the pigmies must think I swallow them or something, and I don't like to disillusion them, in case – well, in case I lost my power over them.'

He laughed and groaned then at the same time, hiding his gaunt beaky face in his hands; the paper-thin skin on his forehead was suddenly showered with sweat. Craig steadied his arm, injected the needle deftly, and rubbed the stringy flesh afterwards.

Standing away from the bed, he said deliberately. 'It's strange the way you stay here on Kakakakaxo when you fear these pigmies so much.'

Daddy Dangerfield looked sharply up, a scarecrow of a man with a shock of hair and a sucked-in mouth. Staring at Craig, his eyes were suddenly very clear, as if he realised for the first time that he was confronted by someone with an awareness of his own. Something like relief crept into his expression. He made no attempt to evade Craig's statement.

'Everyone who goes into space has a good reason driving them,' he said; 'you don't only need escape velocity, you need a private dream – or a private nightmare.' As always he spoke in Galingua, using it stiffly and unemphatically. 'Me, I could never deal with people; it's always been one of my troubles; perhaps that was one of the reasons why I was touchy when you arrived. Human beings – you never know where you stand with them. I'd rather face death with the pigmies than life with humanity. There's a confession for you, Hodges, coming from Far-Flung Father Dangerfield. . . . Maybe all heroes are just escapees, if you could see into them, right into the core of them.'

The injection was taking effect. His words were coming more slowly.

'. . . So I stay on here, God of the guts,' he said. His laugh wrecked itself on a shoal of wheezes; clutching his chest, he lay back.

He hunched himself up in a foetal position, breathing heavily. The bed creaked, and in a moment he was asleep. Craig sat quite still, his face expressionless, integrating all he had learnt or guessed about Dangerfield, without entirely realising what he was doing. At last he shrugged, rose, and slipped the PEST harness from his shoulders; unzipping a pouch, he extracted two specimen jars. Standing them on the table, he poured the bloody contents of the mud bowls one into one jar, one into the other. He set down the bowls, stoppered up the jars, and returned them to his pack.

'That solves his worry about disposing of the tribute for today,' Craig said aloud. 'And now, I think, a little helminthology.'

As he returned through the village, he noticed that several pigmies lay motionless on the ground, glaring unwinkingly at each other over the two lacerated heaps of fur. Circling them, he entered the overlander. It was unexpectedly good to breathe air free from fish.

'I think I've broken the ice with Dangerfield,' he announced to Barney and Tim. 'He's sleeping now. I'll go back over there in a couple of hours, to try and treat his "fiffin", and get him in a proper frame of mind for talking. Before that, let's eat; my stomach grows vociferous.'

'How about exploring the temple in the cliff, Craig?' Tim asked.

Craig smiled. 'If it *is* a temple,' he said. 'We'll let it keep till the morning. We don't want to upset the locals more than possible: though I admit they're a pretty phlegmatic lot, they might well take umbrage at our barging in there. And by morning, I'm hoping Dangerfield will have given us more to go on.'

Over the meal, Barney told Craig of two weaver birds he and Tim had snared while Craig was with Dangerfield.

'The younger one had about one thousand six hundred lice on it,' he said. 'Not an unusually large number for a bird living in a colony, and a youngster at that, not yet expert at preening. It goes to show that the usual complex ecological echelons are in full swing on Kakakakaxo.'

When they had eaten, drunk some of Barney's excellent Aldebaran wine and were lingering over the coffee, Tim volunteered to go over and sit with Dangerfield.

'Excellent idea,' Craig agreed, gratefully. 'I'll be over to relieve you when I've done some work here. On your way, take a look at what the pigmies in the clearing are up to. And be careful – night's coming.'

Collecting his kit and torch Tim went out. Barney returned to his birds. Craig closeted himself in the tiny lab with his jars of entrails.

* * *

Outside, curtains of night drew across the sky with sad finality. Tim zipped up his jacket. Striking through the grass a yard away from him passed a lithe serpent resembling the fer-de-lance, that deadly snake with the beautiful name. It ignored Tim. Cassivelaunus was sinking below the western horizon. Beneath the sheltering trees, darkness was already dominant: a fish scale gleamed here and there like a muddy star. The weavers were settling to roost, making a perpetual uneasy noise overhead. Kept apart by their tethers, peke and bear lay staring at each other in disconsolate pairs, indifferent to day and night. Hardly a pigmy moved; joylessly they lay beneath their crude shelters, not sleeping, not watching.

Five pigmies lay in the open. These were the ones Craig had noticed earlier. As he made his way across the clearing, Tim saw that they were waiting, two round one body, three round the other body of the two creatures who had recently been sacrificed.

They crouched tensely about the two little bundles of battered fur, glaring at one another, not moving as Tim skirted them.

In Dangerfield's hut, he found the overturned oil lamp and a jar of fish oil to refill it with. He trimmed the wick and lit it. Though it gave off a reek of fish, he preferred it to the glare of his own atomic torch. Dangerfield was sleeping peacefully. Tim covered the old man with a blanket, settling down beside him.

Over him moved a feeling of wonder, or perhaps it was what Barney had called 'the occult sense of secrecy' emanating from an unknown planet. Tim experienced it with the strange sense man still does not officially recognise; and the vast barriers of space, the glaciers of Kakakakaxo, and the old hermit sleeping with a head stuffed full of untapped knowledge were all part of it. He experienced nothing of Craig's dislike of altering the nature of a planet, but suddenly he felt impatient for the morning, when they would integrate and interpret the riddles they glimpsed around them.

A succession of leathery blows sounded outside, rousing him from his reverie.

Jumping up, seizing his blaster, Tim stared out into the fishy shadows of the clearing. In the thick silence, the noises were crude and startling.

The three cayman-heads who had crouched over one of the mutilated pelts were fighting. They fought voicelessly, with terrible skill. Though they were small, they battled like giants. Their main weapons were their long jaws, which they wielded as deftly as rapiers, parrying, thrusting, slashing, biting. When their jaws became wedged together in temporary deadlock, they used their barbed paws. Each fought against the other two.

After some five minutes of this murderous activity, the three fell down again, collapsing with their faces on the ground, to eye each other motionlessly once more over the body of the sacrificed bear.

A little later, the two pigmies crouched over the dead peke rose and also did battle, a ferocious duel ending with a sudden reversion into immobility. However much any of the five pigmies suffered from any wounds they received in the engagements, they gave no sign of pain.

'They are fighting over the gutted bodies of their slaves.'

Tim turned from the window. Dangerfield had roused, woken by the thumping outside. He spoke tiredly, without opening his eyes. By a quirk of the dim lighting, his eye sockets and the hollows of his cheeks looked like deep holes.

'What are they fighting for?' Tim asked, instinctively dropping his voice.

'Every night they fight in the same way.'

'But *why*?'

'Tenacity . . . fight to the death. . . . Sometimes goes on all night,' the old man muttered. His voice trailed off.

'What does it all mean?' Tim asked, but Dangerfield had drifted back into sleep, and the question faded unanswered into the darkness. For an hour, the old man slept undisturbedly. Then he became restless, throwing off his blanket and tearing open his shirt, although it had grown chilly in the room. Tossing on the bed, he clawed repeatedly at his chest, couching and groaning.

Bending over him anxiously, Tim noticed a patch of discoloured skin under one of the sick man's ribs. A small red spot was growing rapidly in size, reddening perceptibly and lopping at the surrounding grey flesh. Dangerfield groaned and cried; Tim caught his wrist helplessly, steadying him against a crisis he could not understand. The growing patch formed a dark centre like a storm cloud. It oozed, then erupted thick blood, which trailed round the circumference of the ribs to soak into the blanket below. In the middle of the tiny, bloody crater, something moved.

A flat, armoured head appeared. It belonged to a small brown larva which now heaved itself into the light, lying exhausted on the discoloured flesh. Overcoming his disgust, Tim pulled a specimen jar from his pack and imprisoned the maggot in it.

'I don't doubt that that's what Dangerfield calls a fiffin,' he said. He discovered his hands were shaking. Sickly, he forced himself to disinfect and dress the hermit's wound. He was still bending over the unconscious man when Craig came in to relieve him, carrying a tape recorder. He was glad to leave before he fainted.

Outside, in the darkness, the five cayman-heads still fought their intermittent, interminable battle. On every plane, Tim thought, endless, meaningless strife continues; he wanted to stop trembling.

*   *   *

The dead hour before the dawn: the time, on any planet in the universe, when the pulse of life falters before once more quickening its beat. Craig, walking a little stiffly, entered the overlander with the tape recorder under his arm. Setting it down, he put coffee on the hotpoint, rinsed his face with cold water, and roused the two sleepers.

'We shall be busy today,' he said, patting the recorder. 'We now have plenty of material to work on – very dubious material, I might add. I have recorded a long talk with Dangerfield, which you must hear.'

'How is he?' Tim asked as he slipped on his tunic.

'Physically, not in bad shape. Mentally, pretty sick. He's a manic-depressive type, I should say. Suddenly he is chummy and communicative, then he's silent and hostile. An odd creature . . .'.

'And the fiffin?'

'Dangerfield thinks it is the larval stage of a dung-beetle, and says they bore through anything. He has had them in his legs before, but this one only just missed his lungs. The pain must have been intense, poor fellow. I gave him a light hypalgesic and questioned him before its effects wore off.'

Barney brought the boiling coffee off the stove, pouring it expertly into three beakers.

'All set to hear the play-back,' he said.

Craig switched the record on. The reels turned slowly, re-creating his voice and Dangerfield's. Barney and Tim sat down to listen: Craig remained standing.

'Now that you are feeling a little better,' Craig-on-tape said, 'perhaps you can give me a few details about life on Kakakakaxo. How much of the language of these so-called pigmies have you been able to pick up? And just how efficiently can they communicate with each other?'

A long silence followed before Dangerfield replied.

'They're an old race, the pigmies,' he said at length. 'Their language has gradually worn down, like an old coin. I've picked up all I can in twenty-odd years, but you can take it from me that most of the time, when they sound as if they're talking, they're just making noises. Nowadays, their language only expresses a few basic attitudes. Hostility. Fear. Hunger. Determination . . .'.

'What about love?' Craig prompted.

'I never heard one of them mention the subject. . . . They're very secretive about sex; I've never seen 'em doing it, and you can't tell male from female. They just lay their eggs in the river mud. . . . What was I saying? . . . Oh yes, about their manner of speech. You've got to remember, Hodges, that I'm the only human – the *only* one – ever to master this clicking they do. When

107

my first would-be rescuers asked me what the natives called this place, I said "kakakakaxo", and now Kakakakaxo it is; that's the name on the star charts and I put it there; it used only to be called Cassivelaunus 1. But I made a mistake, as I found later, "Kakakakaxo" is the pigmy answer to the question "Where is this place?"; it means "where we die, where our elders died".'

'Have you been able to explain to them where you came from?'

'That's a bit difficult for them to grasp. They've settled for "Beyond the ice".'

'Meaning the glaciers to the north and south of this equatorial belt?'

'Yes; that's why they think I'm a god, because only gods can live beyond the ice. The pigmies know all about the glaciers. I've been able to construct a bit of their history from similar little items —'

'That was one of the next things I was going to ask you about,' Craig-on-tape said, as Barney-in-the-flesh handed round more coffee to the other two listeners.

'The pigmies are an ancient race,' old Dangerfield said. 'They've no written history, of course, but you can tell they're old by their knowing about the glaciers. How would equatorial creatures know about glaciers, unless their race survived the last Ice Age? Then this ornamented cliff in which many of them live . . . they could build nothing like that now: they haven't the skill. Their ancestors must have been really clever. These contemporary generations are just decadent.'

After a brief silence, Craig's voice came sceptically from the loudspeaker: 'We had an idea that the temple might have been built by another, vanished race. Any opinions on that?'

'You've got the wrong end of the stick, Hodges. The pigmies look on this temple as sacred; somewhere in the middle of it is what they refer to as "the Tomb of the Old Kings", and even *I* have never been allowed in there. They wouldn't behave like that if the place hadn't a special significance for them.'

'Do they still have kings now?'

'No. They don't have any sort of rule now, except each man for himself. These five of them fighting outside the hut, for instance; there's nobody to stop them, so they'll go on until they are all dead.'

'Why should they fight over the pelts?'

'It's a custom, that's all. They do it every night; sometimes one of them wins quickly, and then it's all over. They sacrifice their slaves in the day and squabble over their bodies at night.'

'Can you tell me why they attach such importance to these little animals – their slaves, as you call them? The relationship between pigmies and slaves has its puzzling aspects.'

'Oh, they don't attach much importance to the slaves. It's just that they make a habit of catching them in the forest, since they regard the pekes and bears as a menace to them; certainly their numbers have increased noticeably since I've been here.'

'Hm. Why do they always keep the two groups separated? Anything significant in that?'

'Why should there be? The pekes and bears are supposed to fight together if they are allowed to intermingle, but whether or not that's true, I can't say. You mustn't expect reasons for everything these pigmies do . . . I mean, they're not rational in the way a man is.'

'As an ecologist, I find there is generally a reason for everything, however obscure that reason may be.'

'You do, do you?' The hermit's tone was pugnacious. 'If you want a reason, you'd better go and find one. All I'm saying is that in nineteen years here, I haven't found one. These pigmies just go by – well, instinct or accident, I suppose.'

Craig reached forward and switched the recorder off. He lit a mescahale and looked searchingly at Barney and Tim. Outside, beyond their heads, he could see the first light pencilling in outlines of trees.

'That's about all that's relevant,' he said. 'The rest of Dangerfield's remarks were mainly autobiographical.'

'What do you make of it, Craig?' Barney Brangwyn asked.

'Before Dangerfield crashed on Kakakakaxo, he was a salesman, a refrigerator salesman, I believe, hopping from one frontier planet to another. He was untrained as an observer.'

'That's so,' Barney agreed. 'You obviously feel as I do: that he has misinterpreted just about everything he has seen, which is easy enough to do on a strange planet, even if you are emotionally balanced. Nothing in his statement can be trusted; it's useless.'

'I wouldn't go so far as to say that,' Craig remarked, with his usual caution. 'It's untrustworthy, yes, but not useless. For instance, he gives us several leads –'

'Sorry, but I'm adrift,' Tim Anderson said, getting up and pacing behind his chair. 'Why should Dangerfield be so wrong? Most of what he said sounded logical enough to me. Even if he had no anthropological or ecological training to begin with, he's had plenty of time to learn.'

'True, Tim, true,' Craig agreed. 'Plenty of time to learn correctly or wrongly. I'm not trying to pass judgement on Dangerfield, but as you know there is hardly a fact in the universe which is not open, at least superficially, to two or more interpretations. Dangerfield's attitude to the pigmies is highly ambivalent, the classical love-hate relationship. He wants to think of them as mere animals, because that would make them less something to be reckoned with; at the same time, he wants to think of them as intelligent beings with a great past, because that makes their acceptance of him as their god the more impressive.'

'And which are the pigmies in reality, animals or intelligent beings?' Tim asked.

Craig smiled mysteriously.

'That is where our powers of observation and deduction come in,' he said.

The remark irritated Tim. Both Craig and Barney could be very uninformative. He turned to leave the overlander, to get away from them both and think things out for himself. As he went out, he remembered the jar with the fiffin lava in it; he had forgotten to place it in the overlander's tiny lab. Not wishing to give Craig cause for complaint, Tim slipped it in now.

Two jars already stood on the lab bench. Tim picked them up and examined them with interest. They contained two dead tapeworms; by the labels on the jars, he saw that Craig had extracted them from the entrails of the animals sacrificed the afternoon before. The cestodes, one of which came from the peke, one from the little bear, were identical: white tapes some twenty-four inches long, with suckers and hooks at the head end. Tim stared at them with interest before leaving the overlander.

Outside, dawn was seeping through the thick trees. He drew the cold air down into his lungs: it was still flavoured with fish. The weaver birds were beginning to call or preen drowsily overhead. A few pigmies were about, moving sluggishly in the direction of the river, presumably in search of breakfast. Tim stood there, shivering slightly with the cold, thinking of the oddity of two diverse species harbouring the same species of tapeworm.

He moved into the clearing. The night-long fight over the dead animals was ended. Of the five pigmies involved, only one remained alive; it lay with the gutted bear in its jaws, unable to move away on account of its injuries. Three of its legs had been bitten off. Tim's horror and compunction dissolved as he saw the whole situation *sub specie aeternitatis*, with cruelty and kindness as mere facets of blind law, with pain and death an inevitable concomitant of life, perhaps he was acquiring something of Craig's outlook.

Possessed by a sudden inspiration, Tim picked up three of the dead pigmies, shouldered them, and staggering slightly under their combined weight, carried them back to the overlander. At the door, he met Craig about to take some breakfast over to Dangerfield.

'Hello,' Craig exclaimed cordially. 'Bringing home the lunch?'

'I thought I'd do a little dissection,' Tim said guardedly. 'Just to see how these creatures work.'

But once in the lab with his burden, he merely donned rubber gloves and slit open the pigmies' stomachs rapidly one by one, paying attention to nothing else. Removing the three intestinal sacs, he found that two of them were badly damaged by worms. Soon he had uncovered half a dozen roundworms, pink in colouration and still alive; they made vigorous attempts with their vestigial legs to climb from the crucible in which he placed them.

He went excitedly into Barney Brangwyn to report his findings. Barney was sitting at the table, manipulating metal rods.

'This contradicts most of the laws of phylogeny,' Tim said, peeling off his gloves. 'According to Dangerfield, the pekes and bears are both recent arrivals on the evolutionary scene here; yet their endoparasites, which Craig has preserved in the lab, are well adapted to their environment inside the creatures, and in all respects resemble the ancient order of tapeworms parasitic in man. The roundworms from the pigmies, on the other hand, bear all the marks of being recent arrivals; they are still something more than virtual egg-factories, they still retain traces of a previous more independent existence – and they cause unnecessary damage to their host, which is always a sign that a suitable status quo has yet to be reached between host and parasite.'

Barney raised his great bushy eyebrows approvingly and smiled at the eagerness on the young man's face.

'Very interesting indeed,' he said. 'What now, Doctor Anderson?'

Tim grinned, struck a pose, and said, in a creditable imitation of Craig's voice, 'Always meditate upon all the evidence, and especially upon those things you do not realise are evidence.'

'Fair enough,' Barney agreed, smiling. 'And while you're

meditating, come and give me a hand on the roof with this patent fishing rod I've made.'

'You have some crazy ideas, Barney; what are you up to now?'

'We're going hunting. Come on! Your worms will keep.'

Getting up, he produced a long, telescopic rod which Tim recognised as one of their spare, collapsible aerials. The last and smallest section was extended, and to it Barney had just finished tying a sharp knife.

'It looks like a gadget for shaving by remote control,' Tim commented.

'Then appearances are deceptive. I'm still hankering after catching myself one of the local pets, without getting bitten into the bargain.'

Climbing up the stepped pole which led into the tiny radio room, Barney undogged the circular observation dome which gave an all-round view of their surroundings. With Tim following closely, he swung himself up and on to the roof of the overlander. He crawled forward on hands and knees.

'Keep down,' he muttered. 'If possible, I'd like this act of folly to go unobserved.'

Under a gigantic tree which spread its boughs over them, they were well concealed. Cassivelaunus was only just breaking through low cloud, and the clearing below was still fairly empty. Lying flat on his stomach, Barney pulled out the sections of aerial until he had a rod several yards long. Steadying this weapon with Tim's aid, he pushed it forward.

The end of it reached to the nearest pigmy shelter. Outside, the two captive animals sat up and watched with interest as the knife descended. The blade hovered over the bear, shifted, and began rubbing gently back and forth across the thong which secured the little animal. In a moment, the thong was severed.

The bear was free. It looked owlishly about, hardly daring to move, and obviously undecided as to what it should do. It scratched its yellow poll in a parody of bewilderment. The neighbouring peke clucked encouragingly at it. At that minute, a procession of pigmies appeared among the trees some distance away, spurring it into action.

Grasping the aerial in its little back hands, the bear swarmed nimbly up it. It jumped on to the overlander roof and stood facing the men, apparently without fear. Barney retracted the aerial as Tim made coaxing noises. Unfortunately, this manoeuvre had been seen from below. A clacking and growling started as pigmies emerged from their shelters and moved towards the overlander.

The alarm had been given by the line of pigmies just emerging from the forest. They wore the look of tired hunters, returning with the dawn. Over their shoulders, trussed with crude thongs, lay freshly caught bears or pekes defeated by their opponent's superior turn of speed. When these pigmies saw what Barney and Tim were about, they dropped their burdens and scuttled at a ferocious pace to the PEST vehicle.

Alarmed by the sudden commotion, the weavers poured from their treetop homes, screeching.

'Let's get in,' Barney said hastily.

Picking up the little bear, which offered no resistance, he swarmed down inside the overlander, closely followed by Tim.

At first the creature was overcome by its new surroundings. It stood on the table and rocked piteously from side to side. Recovering, it accepted milk and chattered to the two men vivaciously. Seen close, it bore little resemblance to a bear, except for its fur covering. It stood upright as the pigmies did, attempting to comb its bedraggled fur with its fingers. When Tim proffered his pocket comb, it used that gratefully, wrenching diligently at the knots in its long coat.

'Well, it's male, it's intelligent, it's quite a little more fetching than its overlords,' commented Tim. 'I hope you won't mind my saying so, Barney, but you have got what you wanted at considerable cost. The wolves are at the door, howling for our blood.'

Looking through the window over Tim's shoulder, Barney saw that the pigmies, in ever-growing numbers, were surrounding the overlander, waving their claws, snapping their jaws. Undoubtedly their ire was roused. They looked, in the blue light, at once repulsive, comic and malign. Barney thought to himself, 'I'm getting to hate those squalid bastards; they've neither mind nor style!'

Aloud he said, 'Sorry we roused them. We seem to have offended against a local law of property, if not propriety. Until they cool down, Craig's return is blocked; he'll have to tolerate Daddy Dangerfield for a while.'

Tim did not reply; before Craig returned, there was something else he wished to do. But first he had to get away from the overlander.

He stood uncertainly behind Barney's back, as the latter lit a mescahale and turned his attention to his new pet. A moment later, Tim climbed up into the radio nest unobserved, opened

113

the dome and stood once more on the roof of the overlander. Catching hold of an overhanging bough, he pulled himself into the big tree; working his way along, screened from the clacking mob below, he got well away from them before dropping down from a lower branch on to clear ground. Then he walked briskly in the direction of the cliff temple.

Dangerfield switched the projector off. As the colours died, he turned eagerly to Craig Hodges.

'There!' he exclaimed, with pride. 'What did you think to that?'

Craig stared at him. Though his chest was still bandaged, the hermit moved about easily. Modern healing treatments had speeded his recovery; he looked ten years younger than the old man who had yesterday suffered from fiffins. The excitement of the film he had just been showing had brought a flush to his cheeks.

'Well, what did you think of it?' he demanded, impatiently.

'I'm wondering what *you* think of it,' Craig said.

Some of the animation left Dangerfield. He looked round the stuffy confines of his hut, as if seeking a weapon. His jaw set.

'You've no respect,' he said. 'I took you for a civilised man, Hodges. But you've no respect, no reverence; you persist in trying to insult me in underhand ways. Even the Droxy film makers recognised me for what I am.'

'I think you mean for what you like to think you are,' Craig said, rising from his rough seat. A heavy stick caught him an unexpected blow on the shoulder; he seized the stick, wrenching it from Dangerfield's grasp and tossing it out of the door.

'Don't do that again,' he warned.

'You insult me! You think I'm mad!' Dangerfield cried.

'I wouldn't go as far as to say that,' Craig said coolly, 'although I confess that your sanity is not of a type that appeals to me.'

Leaving the hut, he made off briskly across the clearing. The first indication Barney had of his return was when the besieging pigmies set up an increased noise outside. Looking through one of the windows of the overlander, Barney could watch Craig approaching; he drew his gun, alert for trouble. The cayman-heads were still in an aggressive mood.

Craig never hesitated. As he drew nearer, part of the rabble detached itself from the overlander and moved towards him, jaws creaking open. Craig ignored them. Without slackening his stride, he pushed through the scaly green bodies. Barney stood rigid with apprehension; he knew that if one of the pigmies

114

moved to the attack, Craig would be finished. The mob would be swarming over him before anyone could save him.

But the pigmies merely croaked excitedly as Craig passed. Jostling, shuffling their paws in the dirt, they let him get by. He mounted the step of the overlander and entered unmolested.

The two men faced each other, Craig reading something of the relief and admiration on Barney's face.

'They must have guessed how stringy I'd taste,' he remarked; and that was all that was said.

He turned his attention to Barney's bear-creature, already christened Fido. The animal chattered perkily as Barney explained how he got it.

'I'll swear Fido has some sort of embryo language,' Barney said. 'In exchange for a good rub down with insecticide, he has let me examine his mouth and throat. He's well enough equipped for speech. His IQ's in good trim, too. Fido's quite a boy.'

'Show him how to use a pencil and paper, and see what he makes of it,' Craig suggested, stroking the little creature's yellow crest.

As Barney did so, he asked Craig what had kept him so long with Dangerfield.

'I was beginning to think the lost race of Kakakakaxo had got you,' he said, grinning.

'Nothing so interesting,' Craig said, 'although it has been an instructive session. Incidentally, I think I may have made an enemy of Dangerfield, under the surface, he resents having had to accept our help. He has been showing me a film intended to impress me with the greatness of Dangerfield.'

'A documentary?'

'Anything but. A squalid solid made by Galactic Studios on Droxy, and supposedly based on the old boy's life. They presented him with a copy of it, and a viewer, as a souvenir. It's called "Curse of the Crocodile Men".'

'Ye Gods!' Barney exclaimed, 'I'll bet you found that instructive.'

'In many ways, it is very helpful,' Craig said seriously. 'The script writers and director spent two days – just two and "soaking up atmosphere", so-called, before returning to Droxy to cook up their own ideas on the subject. No other research was done.'

Barney laughed briefly. 'I presume the result was phoney through and through?'

'Absolutely false. After the usual preliminaries – spectacular spaceship crash on mountainside, etcetera – a Tarzan-like

115

Dangerfield is shown being captured by the bear-race, who stand six feet high and wear tin helmets. The pekes, for simplicity's sake, never appear. The bears are torturing our hero to death when the Crocodile Men, the pigmies, raid the place and rescue him. The Crocodile Men, according to the film, are a proud and ancient warrior race, come down in the world through the encroachment of the jungle. When they get Dangerfield, they don't like him. They, too, are about to put him to death when he saves the leader's son from foot-rot or something equally decisive. From then on, the tribe treats him like a god, build him a palace and all the rest of it. Appalling, "B" feature stuff, full of fake dialogue and settings.'

'Hm, I see,' Barney said. He sat silent for a minute, looking rather puzzledly into space, tweaking his beard. 'It is odd that, considering this hokum was cooked up on Droxy, it all tallies surprisingly well in outline with what Dangerfield told us last night about the great past of the pigmies and so on.'

'Exactly!' Craig agreed with satisfaction. 'Don't you see what that means, Barney? Nearly everything Dangerfield knows, or believes he knows, comes from a hack in a Droxy studio, rather than vice versa.'

They stared at one another, Barney rather blankly. Into both their minds, like the faint sound of a hunter's horn, came the reflection that all human behaviour, ultimately, is inexplicable; even the explicable is a mystery.

'Now you see why he shied away from us so violently at our first meeting.' Craig said. 'He's got almost no first-hand information because he is afraid to go out looking for it. Knowing that, he was prepared to face Droxy film people – who would only be after a good story – but not scientists, who would want hard facts. Once I had him cornered, of course, he had to come out with what he'd got, presumably hoping we would swallow it as the truth and go.'

Barney made clucking noises. 'He's probably no longer fit to remember what is truth, what lies. After nineteen years alone here the old boy must be quietly crazy.'

'Put the average person, with the mental conflicts to which we are all prey, away on an unlovely planet like Kakakakaxo for nineteen years,' Craig said, 'and he will inevitably finish as some sort of fantasist. I don't say insane, for a human mind is very resilient, but shielded away from reality. Fear has worked steadily on Dangerfield all this time. He's afraid of people, afraid of the cayman-heads, the Crocodile Men. He hides from his terrors in fantasy. He's a "B" feature god. And you couldn't budge him off the planet because he realises subconsciously that reality would then catch up with him.'

Barney stood up.

'Okay, doctor,' he said. 'Diagnosis accepted. All we have collected so far are phantoms. Now just tell me where exactly PEST work stands after this revelation of the uselessness of our main witness. Presumably, at a standstill?'

'By no means,' Craig said. He pointed to Fido. The little bear was sitting quietly on the table with the pencil in his hand, licking the point with nonchalance.

On the paper, he had crudely drawn a room, in which a bear and a peke were locked in each other's arms, as if wrestling.

A few minutes later, when Craig had gone into the laboratory with some beetles and other insects culled from Dangerfield's hut, Barney saw the old hermit himself coming across to them, hobbling rapidly among the pigmy shelters with the aid of a stick. Barney called to Craig.

Craig emerged from the lab with a curious look on his face, at once pleased and secretive.

'Those three pigmy carcasses which Tim brought into the lab,' he said. 'I presume Tim cut them up – it certainly doesn't look like your work. What did he say to you about them?'

Barney explained the point Tim had made about the worms. 'Is there anything wrong?' he inquired.

'No, nothing, nothing,' Craig said in an odd voice, shaking his head. 'And that's all Tim said. . . . Where is he now by the way?'

'I've no idea, Craig; the boy's getting as secretive as you are. He must have gone outside for a breath of fish. Shall I give him a call?'

'Let's tackle Dangerfield first,' Craig said.

They opened the door. Most of the pigmies had dispersed. The rest of them sped away when Dangerfield waved to them. The old man agitatedly refused to come into the overlander, his great nose standing out from his head like a parrot's beak as he shook his head. He wagged a finger angrily at them.

'I always knew no good would come of your nosing about here,' he said. 'It was foolish of me to condescend to have anything to do with you in the first place. Now that young fellow of yours is being killed by the pigmies, and serve him right, too. But goodness knows what they'll do when they've tasted human flesh – tear us all apart, I shouldn't wonder. I doubt if I'll be able to stop them, for all my power over them.'

117

He had not finished talking before Craig and Barney had leapt from the overlander.

'Where's Tim? What's happened to him?' Craig asked. 'Tell us straightforwardly what you know.'

'Oh, I expect it'll be too late now,' said Dangerfield. 'I saw him slip into the cliff temple, the interfering young fool. Perhaps you will go away now and leave me –'

But the two PEST men were already running across the clearing, scattering brilliant birds about their heads. They jumped the crude shelters in their path. As they neared the temple in the cliff, they heard the monotonous clacking of the pigmy pack. When they reached the ornamental doorway, they saw that it and the corridor beyond were packed tight with the creatures, all fighting to get further into the cliff.

'Tim!' bawled Barney. 'Tim! Are you here?'

The clacks and croaks died instantly. The nearer pigmies turned to stare at the men, swinging their green snouts inquisitively round. In the silence, Barney shouted again, but no answer came. The mob continued its struggle to get into the temple.

'We can't massacre this lot,' Craig said, glaring at the mob of cayman-heads before them. 'How're we going to get in there to Tim?'

'We can use the cry gas in the overlander!' Barney said. 'That will shift the pigmies.' He doubled back to their vehicle, and in a minute brought it bumping and growling across the clearing towards the temple. It was tough going. The high roof ploughed through overhanging trees, breaking down the weavers' carefully constructed roof and sending angry birds flying in all directions. As the vehicle lumbered up, Craig unstrapped an outside container, pulling out a hose; the other end of it was already connected to internal gas tanks. Barney threw down two respirators, to emerge a moment later wearing one himself.

Donning his mask, Craig slung the spare over his arm and charged forward with the hose. The reeking gas poured over the nearest pigmies, who fell back like magic, coughing and pawing at their goat-yellow eyes. The two men entered the temple; they moved down the corridor unopposed, only impeded by the pigmies' wild flight to get out of their way. The noise of croaking was tremendous; in the dark and mist, Craig and Barney could hardly see their way ahead.

The corridor changed into a pigmy-sized tunnel, working gently upwards through the mountain. The two ecologists had to struggle past kicking bodies. It occurred to Craig that the

118

pigmies, for a tribe of savages little higher than brutes, had behaved fairly phlegmatically until now. But now they were confronting cry gas; they could not comprehend it, and they were really frightened.

The supply of cry gas gave out. Craig and Barney stopped, peering at each other in surprise and some apprehension.

'I thought the gas tanks were full?' Craig said.

'They were. One of the cayman-heads must have unwittingly bitten through the hose.'

'Or Dangerfield cut it . . .'.

Dropping the now useless hose, they ran forward. Their retreat was cut off: the pigmies at the mouth of the temple would have recovered by now, and be waiting for the men to return. So they forged ahead, both throwing off their respirators and pulling out blaster-guns as they turned a corner.

There they stopped. This was the end of the trail. The tunnel broadened into a sort of ante-room, on the opposite side of which stood a wide wooden door. A group of pigmies who had been scratching at this door – its panels were deeply marked by their claws – turned and confronted the men. Tears, crocodile tears, stood in their eyes: a whiff of the gas had reached them, but it had served only to anger them. Six of them were there. They charged. There was no avoiding them.

'Get 'em!' Barney yelled.

The dim chamber twitched with blinding blue-white light. Blue hieroglyphs writhed on the wall. Acoustics, in the roar of the blasters, went crazy. But the best hand weapon has its limitations, and the pigmies had speed on their side. Terrifying speed. They launched themselves like stones from a sling.

Barney scarcely had time to settle one of them than another landed squarely in his stomach. For a small creature, it was unbelievably solid. Every claw dug a point of pain through Barney's thick suit. He jerked his head back, falling backwards, bellowing, as the jaws gaped up to his face. Its grey tongue, its serried teeth, the stink of fish – he tried to writhe away from them as he fired the blaster against the pigmy's leathery stomach. Even as he hit the ground, the pigmy fell from him, dead, and in a dying kick knocked the weapon from his hand.

Before Barney could reach it, two other assailants had landed on him, sending him sprawling. He was defenceless under their predatory claws.

The blue light leapt and crackled over him. An intolerable heat breathed above his cheek. The two pigmies rolled over to

119

lie beside him, their bodies black and charred. Shakily, Barney stood up.

The wooden door had been flung open. Tim was there, holstering the blaster which had saved Barney's life.

Craig had settled with his two attackers. They lay twitching and smouldering on the floor in front of him. He stood now, breathing deeply, with only a torn tunic sleeve to show for his trouble. The three men looked at each other, grimed and dishevelled. Craig was the first to speak.

'I'm getting too old for this sort of lark,' he said.

'I thought we'd had it then; thanks a lot, Tim,' Barney said.

His beard had been singed, its edges turned a dusty brown. He felt his cheek tenderly where a blister was already forming. Sweat poured from him; the heat from the thermonuclear blasts had considerably raised the temperature in the ante-room.

'Why did I ever leave Earth?' he growled, stepping over one of the scaly corpses.

'You got yourself into a nasty spot,' Craig said to Tim. The young man instantly became defensive, looking both embarrassed and defiant.

'I'm sorry you came in after me,' he said. 'I was quite safe behind this door, as it happened. I've been doing a little research on my own. Craig — you'd better come in and see this place for yourself, now that you're here. I have discovered the Tomb of the Old Kings that Dangerfield told us about! You'll find it explains quite a lot we did not know.'

'How did you manage to get as far as this without the pigmies stopping you?' Craig asked, still stern.

'There was a diversion on when I entered. Most of them were clustered round the overlander. They only started creeping up on me when I was actually inside. Are you coming in or aren't you?'

They entered, Tim barring the door behind them before turning to pick out the details of the long room with his torch beam. The proportions of the place were agreeable. Despite its low roof, it was architecturally impressive. Its builders had known what they were doing. Decoration had been left at a minimum, except for the elaborate door arch and the restrained fan-vaulting of the ceiling. Attention was thus focused on a large catafalque, upon which lay a row of several sarcophagi. They had a pathetic, neglected look. Everywhere was deep in dust, and the air tasted stale and heavy.

120

Tim pointed to the line of little coffins, the outsides of which were embellished with carvings.

'Here are the remains of the Old Kings of Kakakakaxo,' he said. 'And although I may have made myself a nuisance, I think I can claim that with their aid I have solved the mystery of the lost race of this planet.'

'Good!' Craig exclaimed encouragingly. 'I should be very interested to hear any deductions you have made.'

For a moment, Tim looked at him penetratingly, suspecting sarcasm. Reassured, he continued.

'The curious thing is that the problem is like a jigsaw puzzle to which we already possessed most of the pieces. Dangerfield supplied nearly all of them – but he had fitted them together upside down. You see, to start with, there is not one lost race but two. This temple – and doubtless others like it all over the planet – was hewn by the races who have engraved their own likenesses on these sarcophagi. Take a look at them! Far from being lost, these two races have been under our noses all the time: I mean of course, the creatures we call pekes and bears. Their potraits are on the sarcophagi and their remains inside. Their resemblance to Earth animals has blinded us to what they really are.'

Tim paused for their approval.

'I'm not surprised,' Barney said, to Tim's regret, turning from an inspection of the stone coffins. 'The bear people at least are brighter than the pigmies. As I see it, the pigmies are pretty stodgy reptiles whom nature has endowed with armour but precious little else. I had already decided that there was another thing Great God Dangerfield had garbled: far from being an ancient race, the pigmies are neoteric, upstart usurpers who have appeared only recently on the scene to oust the peke and bear people. Any knowledge of the glaciers they may have is, of course, because they drifted down from the cold regions until the river brought them to these equatorial lands. As for the bear people – and I suspect the same goes for the pekes – their chatter, far from being the beginning of a language, is the decadent tail-end of one. They're the ancient races, already in decline when the parvenu pigmies descended on them.'

'The helminthological evidence supports this theory.' Tim said eagerly. 'The cayman-heads are too recent to have developed their own peculiar cestodes; they were almost as much harmed by interior parasites, the roundworms, as was Daddy by his fiffin. As you know, in a long-established hostparasite relationship, the amount of internal damage is minimal.'

'As was the case with the peke and bear cestodes I uncovered,' Craig agreed.

'Directly I saw these roundworms, I realised that Dangerfield's claim that the pigmies were the ancient species and their "pets" the new might be the very reverse of the truth. I came over here at once, hoping to find proof: and here it is.'

'It was a good idea, Tim,' Barney said heartily, 'but you shouldn't have done it alone – far too risky.'

'The habit of secretiveness is catching.' Tim said.

He looked challengingly at Craig, but the chief ecologist seem not to have heard the remark, striding grimly over to the door and putting an ear to it. Barney and Tim listened too. The noise was faint at first; then it was unmistakable, a chorus of guttural grunts and croaks. The cry gas had dispersed. The pigmies were pressing back into the temple.

Almost visibly, this sound took on depth and volume. It rose to a sudden climax as claws struck the outside of the door. Craig stood back. The door shook. A babel of noise revealed that the pigmies had arrived in strength.

'This is not a very good place in which to stay,' Craig said, turning back to the other two. 'Is there another exit?'

Hastily, they moved down the long room. Its walls were blank. Behind them, urging them on, the wooden door rattled and groaned dangerously. At the far end, a screen stood. Behind it, two steps up to a narrow door. When Barney tried it, it would not open. With one thrust of his great shoulders, Barney sent it shattering back. Rusted hinges and lock left a red, bitter powder floating on the air. Climbing over the door, they found themselves in a steep and narrow tunnel, so small that they were forced to go one ahead of the other.

'I should hate to be caught in here,' Tim said. 'Do you think the pigmies will actually dare to enter the tomb-room? They seem to regard it as sacred.'

'Their blood's up. A superstition will hardly bother them,' said Barney.

Still Tim hesitated.

'What I still don't understand,' he said, 'is why the pigmies care so much for the temple if it has nothing to do with them.'

'You probably never will,' Craig said. 'The temple must be a symbol of their new dominance for them and one man's symbol is another man's enigma. I can hear that door splintering; let's get up this tunnel. It looks like a sort of priest's bunk-hole – it must lead somewhere.'

One behind the other, Barney leading, they literally crawled along the shaft. It bore steadily upwards at an angle of forty-five degrees for what seemed like miles. They seemed to crawl for ever. On all sides, the mountain made its presence felt, dwarfing them, threatening them, as if they were cestodes working their way up a vast alimentary canal.

The shaft at last turned upwards still more steeply. They had climbed at this new and more difficult angle for some while when Barney stopped.

'The way's blocked!' he exclaimed.

In the confined space, it sounded almost like a death sentence.

Tim shone the torch. The tunnel was neatly stoppered with a solid substance. 'Rock fall!' he whispered.

'We can't use a blaster on it in this space,' Barney said, 'or we'll cook or suffocate.'

Craig passed a knife forward.

'Try the blockage with this,' he said, 'and see what it's made of.'

The stopper flaked reluctantly as Barney scraped. They examined the flakes; Tim recognised them first.

'This is guano – probably from bats!' he exclaimed. 'We must be very near the surface. Thank goodness for that!'

'It's certainly guano,' Craig agreed, 'but it's almost as hard as stone with age. Look, a limestone shell has formed over the bottom of it: it must be thousands of years old. There may be many feet of guano between us and the surface.'

'Then we'll have to dig through it,' Barney said.

There was no alternative. It was an unpleasant task. The ill-smelling guano rapidly became softer as they dug, until it reached the consistency of moist cake. They rolled lumps of it back between their knees, sending it bounding back, down into the mountain. It clung stickily to them, and emphasised the parallel between their situation and a cestode in an alimentary canal. They stuck at it grimly, wishing they had kept their respirators.

Twenty-five feet of solid guano had to be tunnelled through before they struck air. Barney's head and shoulders emerged into a small cave. A wild dog-like creature backed growling into the open and ran for safety. It had taken over this cave for a lair long after the bats had deserted it. When Barney had climbed out, the other two followed, standing blinking in the intense blue light. They were plastered with filth. Hardly uttering a word to each other, they left the cave and took great breaths of fresh air.

Trees and high bushes surrounded them. The ground sloped steeply down to the left, so they began to descend in that direction. They were high up the mountainside; Cassivelaunus gleamed through the leaves above them.

'Thank goodness there's nothing else to keep us any longer on Kakakakaxo,' Barney said at last. 'We just file our report to PEST HQ, and we're off. Dangerfield will be glad to see the back of us. I wonder how he'll like the colonists? They'll come flocking in in no time once HQ gets our clearance. Well, there's nothing here the biggest fool can't handle.'

'Except Dangerfield,' Craig added.

'The man with the permanent wrong end of the stick!' Tim said, laughing. 'He will probably see out his days selling the colonists signed picture postcards of himself.'

They emerged from the trees suddenly. Before them was a cliff, steep and bush-studded. The ecologists went to its edge and looked down.

A fine panorama stretched out before them. Far in the distance, perhaps fifty miles away, a range of snow-covered mountains seemed to hang suspended in the blue air. Much nearer at hand, winding between mighty stetches of jungle, ran the cold, wide river. On the river banks, the ecologists could see the lumpy bodies of pigmies, basking in the sun; in the water, others swam and dived, performing miracles of agility.

'Look at them!' Craig exclaimed. 'They are really aquatic creatures. They've hardly had time to adapt properly to land life. The dominating factor of their lives remains – fish!'

'And they've already forgotten all about us,' Barney said.

They could see the crude settlement was deserted. The overlander was partially discernible through the trees, but it took them an hour of scrambling down hazardous paths before they reached it. Never had the sight of it been more welcome.

Craig went round to look at the severed cry gas hose. It had been neatly chopped, as if by a knife. Obviously, this was Dangerfield's work; he had expected to trap them in the temple. There was no sign of the old man anywhere. Except for the melancholy captives, sitting at the end of their tethers, the clearing was deserted.

'Before we go, I'm setting these creatures free,' Barney said.

He ran among the shelters, slashing at the thongs with a knife, liberating the pekes and the bears. As soon as they found themselves loose, they banded together and trotted off into the jungle

124

without further ado. In a minute they were gone.

'In another two generations,' Barney said regretfully, 'there probably won't be a bear or a peke on Kakakakaxo alive outside a zoo; the colonists will make shorter work of them than the cayman-heads have. As for the cayman-heads, I don't doubt they'll only survive by taking to the rivers again.'

'There's another contradiction,' Tim remarked thoughtfully, as they climbed into the overlander and Barney backed her again through the trees. 'Dangerfield said the peke and bear people fought with each other if they had the chance, yet they went off peacefully enough together – and they ruled together once. Where does the fighting come in?'

'As you say, Dangerfield always managed to grab the wrong end of the stick,' Craig answered. 'If you take the opposite of what he told us, that's likely to be the truth. He has always been too afraid of his subjects to go out and look for the truth.'

'And I suppose he just doesn't use his eyes properly,' Tim remarked innocently.

'None of us do,' Craig said. 'Even you, Tim!'

Barney laughed.

'Here it comes,' he said. 'I warn you, the oracle is about to speak, Tim! In some ways you're very transparent, Craig; I've known ever since we left the Tomb of the Old Kings that you had something up your sleeve and were just waiting for an appropriate moment before you produced it.'

'What is it, Craig?' Tim asked curiously.

Barney let Fido out of the overlander; the little creature hared off across the clearing with one brief backward wave, running to catch up its fellows.

'You were careless when you opened those three pigmies in the lab, Tim,' Craig said gently. 'I know that you were looking for something else, but if you had been less excited, you would have observed that the cayman-heads are parthenogenic. They have only one sex, reproducing by means of unfertilized eggs.'

Just for a minute, Tim's face was a study in emotion, then he said in a small voice. 'How interesting! But does this revelation make any practical difference to the situation?'

Barney had no such inhibitions. He smote his forehead in savage surprise.

'Ah, I should have seen it myself! Parthenogenic, of course! Self-fertilising! It's the obvious explanation of the lack of vanity or sexual inhibition which we noticed, I swear I would have hit on the answer myself, if I hadn't been so occupied with Fido and Co.'

He climbed heavily into the driver's seat, slamming the door. The air-conditioning sucked away the invading smell of fish at once.

'Yes, you have an interesting situation on Kakakakaxo,' Craig continued. 'Try and think how different it would be for such a parthenogenic species to visualise a bi-sexual species like man. The concept would probably be beyond them; it is easier for us to visualise a four-dimensional race. Nevertheless, the pigmies managed to do something of the sort – they're not so foolish as you may have thought, for all their limitations. What is more, they grasped the one fatal weakness of the bi-sexual system: that if you keep the two sexes apart, the race dies out. So without quite realising what they were doing, they did just that, separating male and female. That is how they manage to hold this place. Of course, no scheme is perfect, and quite a few of both sexes escaped into the forest to breed there.'

Barney revved the engine, moving the overlander forward, leaving Tim to ask the obvious question.

'Yes,' Craig said. 'As Fido tried to explain to us, the "bears" are males, the "pekes" the females of *one* species. It just happens to be an extremely dimorphous species, the sexes varying in size and configuration, or we would have guessed the truth at once. The pigmies, in their dim way, knew. They tackled the whole business of conquest in a new way that only a parthenogenic race would think of – they segregated the sexes. That is how they managed to supercede the intellectually superior peke-bear race: by applying the old law of "Divide and conquer" in a new way! I'm now trying to make up my mind whether that is crueller or kinder, in the long run, than slaughter. . . .'

Tim whistled.

'So when Dangerfield thought the pekes and bears were fighting,' he said, 'they were really making love! And of course the similar cestodes you found in their entrails would have given you the idea; I ought to have twigged it myself!'

'It must be odd to play God to a world about which you really know or care so little,' Barney commented, swinging the big vehicle down the track in the direction of their spaceship.

'It must be indeed,' Craig agreed, but he was not thinking of Dangerfield.

*   *   *

126

The old man hid behind a tree, silently watching the overlander leave. He shook his head sadly, braced himself, hobbled back to his hut. His servants would have to hunt in the jungles before he got today's offering of entrails. He shivered as he thought of those two symbolic and steaming bowls. He shivered for a long time. He was cold; he was old: from the sky he had come; to the sky he would one day return. But before that, he was going to tell everyone what he really thought of them.

Going to tell them how he hated them.

How he despised them.

How he needed them.

NEL BESTSELLERS